RECIPE

FOR

MURDER

by

KEN FARMER & BUCK STIENKE

Cover Art
Adriana Girolami
K. R. Farmer

AUTHOR

Ken Farmer didn't write his first full novel until he was sixty-nine years of age. He often wonders what the hell took him so long. At age seventy-seven...he's currently working on novel number thirty. Ken spent thirty years raising cattle and quarter horses in Texas and forty-five years as a professional actor (after a stint in the Marine Corps). Those years gave him a background for storytelling...or as he has been known to say, "I've always been a bit of a bull---t artist, so writing novels kind of came naturally once it occurred to me I could put my stories down on paper."

Ken's writing style has been likened to a combination of Louis L'Amour and Terry C. Johnston with an occasional Hitchcockian twist...now that's a combination.

In addition to his love for writing fiction, he likes to teach acting, voice-over and writing workshops. His favorite expression is: "Just tell the damn story."

Writing has become Ken's second life: he has been a Marine, played collegiate football, been a Texas wildcatter, cattle and horse rancher, professional film and TV actor and director, and now...a novelist. Who knew?

Ken Farmer's dialogue flows like a beautiful western river...it's the gold standard...Carole Beers

Web page: www.KenFarmer-Author.net

THE AUTHOR

Buck Stienke is a Texas native from Houston. He moved to the central Texas hill country when he was ten and found the rural lifestyle more to his liking.

He graduated from the USAF Academy with a BS in Engineering Management. Buck flew single and multi-engine jets and multi-engine recip aircraft for the US Air Force before embarking on a twenty five year commercial airline career that took him to Asia, South America, North America, Central America, Hawaii, Bermuda, the Caribbean, the Middle East and Europe.

In addition to aviation, his widely varied interests have included ranching, professional football player, gourmet cooking, movie producer, singer / songwriter, sporting goods retailer, big game hunting, gunsmith, machinist, and designer of suppressors. Each of these interests are reflected in his writings.

To date, Buck has written or co-written and released eighteen titles. Ten are in the Black Eagle Force series, four are in The Nations series or Flynn spinoffs, and four are independent titles.

His latest, *Bone's Paradox* is a police procedural /sci fi tale involving characters that appear in both The Black Eagle Force and The Nations.

ISBN-13: 978-1-7341765-1-3

Timber Creek Press
Imprint of Timber Creek Productions, LLC
312 N. Commerce St.
Gainesville, Texas 76240

Published by: Timber Creek Press
timbercreekpresss@yahoo.com
www.timbercreekpress.net
Twitter: @pagact
Facebook Book Page:
www.facebook.com/TimberCreekPress
Ken's email: pagact@yahoo.com
214-533-4964

DEDICATION

We would like to dedicate this tome to our acting students who served as inspirations for some of our characters. Eryn Brooke as Corporal Stella Johnson, Brandi D'Aun Price as Peach Presley, Kelly O. Jackson as Captain St. John and in memoriam, Maeghan Albach 1974 - 2019 - as Corporal Wanda Stanton. May she rest in peace…she was a sweet soul and we loved her dearly.

ERYN BROOKE
as **STELLA JOHNSON**

BRANDI D'AUN PRICE
as **PEACH PRESLEY**

KELLY O. JACKSON
as **CAPTAIN ST. JOHN**

MAEGHAN ALBACH
as **WANDA STANTON**

ACKNOWLEDGMENT

The author gratefully acknowledges Lt. Colonel Clyde DeLoach, USMC (Ret.), Terry Heflin - retired English Professor at Tarrant County College, and award-winning, best-selling novelist Mary Deal, for their invaluable help in proofing, beta reading and editing this novel.

TIMBER CREEK PRESS

CHAPTER ONE

COOKE COUNTY, TEXAS
OCT. 27, 2014

"Told you needed to start earlier…already warmin' up…Deer'll be beddin' down." Jim Bob Owenby pushed a head high branch sticking out from a small chinkapin oak sapling out of the way.

"Hell, practically had to sneak out as it was…You know how Sara is about huntin'…Damn, what's that smell?" Ernie Owenby sniffed the air.

The brothers were almost to their bow stands in Frog Bottom in the heavily wooded Red River valley in the northern part of the county.

Jim Bob sniffed the crisp morning fall air. "Somethin' dead…Probably a deer somebody gut shot and couldn't find…" He pointed. "Comin' from over there."

They walked over to a copse of dogwood saplings. Ernie kicked some of the new fallen leaves aside, and then jumped back, stumbling, to fall on his rear.

"Oh, Jesus Christ! Jesus Christ amighty!"

"Oh, God!" Jim Bob bent over and upchucked his breakfast as he saw the light brown woman's hand, curled almost into a claw, sticking out from under the leaves.

GAINESVILLE, TEXAS

Corporal Stella Johnson, a drop dead gorgeous blonde police officer, wheeled her black and gold squad car into the Radio Hut retail store in a strip mall north of Texas Highway 82. She found a parking spot near the front door, pulled in and turned off the ignition of the older Ford Victoria.

She scanned the area around the store briefly, stepped out and locked the patrol unit before heading into the small shop.

The large, broad shouldered, thirty year old sales clerk looked up as she walked in and removed her dark Ray Bans. Her shoulder length ponytail danced around as she scanned the aisles for the radio controlled cars.

He stood a little taller as a smile came to her lips.

"See something you like, Miss?"

She glanced at his name tag. "Yeah, Mister Lipschitz…"

"Just call me Bernie, Miss."

Stella nodded. "Well, Bernie, think I found the right area…He told me what to look for…" She looked up at his 6'5" height. "Wow, you're almost as big as one of our detectives. What do you weigh…'bout 300 pounds?"

He blushed and looked at his feet. "Yes, ma'am…Pretty close."

Stella walked past him. His eyes never moved from her—the navy blue duty uniform did absolutely nothing to hide her voluptuous hourglass figure—not even the Sam Brown belt complete with a Glock 17, extra mags, cuffs, Stun Gun, and tactical radio.

"We have a great selection, you know…With Christmas shopping starting in a couple of weeks."

"Some folks wait for seasonal sales…not me." Stella shook her head.

Some of the Remote Control cars were Camaros, others stylized fastbacks resembling Mustangs. There were high-lift pickup trucks and Jeeps, but her eyes spotted a desert camo Hummer about the size of a shoebox.

"Bingo." She picked up the box, quickly read the label and nodded.

When she set the box down on the counter, the clerk grinned.

"Great selection, Ma'am…For your son?"

"Nope. Single…no kids…Don't even have a dog." Stella flashed a dazzling smile. "For a friend."

"Cool…that be all for you?"

"It'll do."

He rang up the sale and glanced at her...name tag. "With tax, total comes to $52.95, Officer Johnson...Cash or credit?"

"Cash. Ya'll still take checks, Bernie?"

"Of course, but have to see your driver's license...company policy, you know." The clerk slipped the toy into a white plastic bag emblazoned with the company logo.

Stella nodded and chuckled as she fished out her check book from a small black purse. "We get to deal with the dummies who try to hang bad paper...DA takes a dim view of those folks."

"I bet."

She ripped the completed check from the burgundy eel skin checkbook and handed it to him. Her driver's license was inside a plastic pouch affixed to the checkbook cover. She held it up for him to copy the license number next to her address on the check.

"Got it."

She snapped the magnetic cover closed and slipped it securely back into her purse. "I know...everybody's goin' to debit cards...Just old fashioned, I suppose."

He nodded as he dropped the receipt into the bag and handed it to her. "Nothing wrong with being a little old fashioned...Fact, nothing wrong with anythin' at all."

His gaze looked her up and down and came to rest on her golden eyes. He was clearly smitten. Her beauty transfixed him for a moment.

Stella blushed, and then she broke into a sheepish grin. "Thanks, I think." She spun around and headed for the door.

GAINESVILLE POLICE DEPARTMENT CRIME INVESTIGATOR'S UNIT

The 6'8" detective handed Stella sixty dollars in twenties. "Here you go, Little Bit. Keep the change...Appreciate the little errand."

"No need...I can never repay you for clearing me of that shooting in CPS."

Bone frowned. "Fool of a DA was a total dipstick for trying to hang that crap on you...Murderin' sumbitch was caught in *flagrante delicto* and then lunged at you. You were in fear for your life...That's the operative phrase, girlfriend. A jury of your peers agreed…Simple as that."

"Never been so scared in all my life. Our Chief was no help and the media…"

Bone held up his hand to stop her. "Vipers and satanists, the lot of 'em. All they want to do is to jack up their stinkin' ratings." He made quote marks in the air. "Cop shoots naked unarmed man…See that all the time." He placed one massive mitt on her slim shoulder. "Say…Aren't you supposed to be on patrol with Gomez?"

"Yeah. Told him to coffee up while I ran your little errand. Question…What are you gonna do with that thing?"

"You don't wanna know. Now get your bubble butt outta here." He grinned and pointed at the door. "Scat."

Stella smiled, shook her head and headed out to find her partner. She passed Loraine on her way in.

"Hey, Stella."

"Mornin', Loraine…might not want to go in there."

The attractive Hispanic Senior Investigator stopped in her tracks. A puzzled look crossed her face. She looked over her shoulder and then back at Bone.

"What are you up to?"

"Nothin'." He took a coonskin cap out of a white plastic bag.

"Playin' Davy Crockett?"

Bone arched one eyebrow and gave her one of his enigmatic looks. "Philistine."

He raised the whip antenna on the roof of the Hummer and threaded it through a small slit that he had made in the top of the cap. He carefully, slipped the furry cap over the radio controlled car, leaving the tail hanging out behind.

Bone admired his creation. "Perfect."

Loraine watched him slide the whole thing back into the white bag. "What in blue blazes are you making? A furbie like on Star Trek?"

"Woman…they were called Tribbles…and the answer is no. St. John in his office?"

"No. Our illustrious captain is in the break room, getting some coffee and hovering over the box of donuts."

"Super." Bone grabbed the modified Hummer, headed for the door and turned down the hall.

Loraine was hot on his heels. "You're not?"

"I am." He looked behind him to check the hallway as he stepped into the Captain's office.

Loraine stood outside as Bone knelt down behind the industrial gray steel desk. "Pard, your bread's not real done."

"So I've been told." He grinned broadly as he slipped the fur covered toy out of the bag and set it toward the far back side of the knee well. Bone made sure it was facing the occupant's chair. He got to his feet crumpled the white bag and stuffed it into his tan-colored tactical cargo pants.

"Come on, girl. Let's motor."

He moved quickly past her.

She took longer steps to try and catch up, but at five feet two inches, that was more than a simple stretch in the stride.

She whispered in a low voice, "What is that thing?"

Bone looked over his shoulder and grinned. He held his index finger up to his lips.

He mouthed the words. "You'll find out."

His cryptic answer did little to assuage her growing curiosity.

She followed him back to their desks—set side by side at the back of the Investigations Unit office.

Bone slipped into his oversized executive chair—one he bought on his own dime to handle 285 pounds of solid muscle and match his oversized frame. He settled back into the padded leather and shot a quick glance at his partner.

Bone's smile could be called, *I know something you don't know.*

Loraine eyed him for a second. "You know, you kinda look like Mona Lisa."

Bone chuckled. "That chick has a lot more hair…but I'm much better lookin'."

"And more modest."

He shook his head. "Modesty is not one of my many virtues."

"I know…You gonna tell me what's up?"

"Negative."

"Why not?"

Bone held up two fingers on his left hand. A rather thin exotic bracelet of turquoise stones with alien symbols inset in pure gold links dangled from his wrist. It looked strangely out of place on a really big man.

"Two words...plausible deniability." He arched one eyebrow.

"Men," Loraine huffed slightly and flipped open her laptop and tried to ignore him.

Bone flipped up his laptop cover but pushed it a bit farther away from the usual position on his desk.

Outside in the hallway, a slightly overweight baldheaded black man walked by with a oversized coffee mug in his right hand. Two chocolate glazed donuts and a light blue napkin filled his left hand.

Captain St. John was dressed in tan 511 slacks, and a black polo shirt with a Gainesville Police Department logo embroidered on the left chest. He sported a Glock 22 in 40 S&W caliber in a saddle colored basket weave holster riding in a Texas Ranger style belt.

He didn't even look into Bone's office as he passed.

A smile came to Bone's face as he slid open the bottom drawer on his desk and retrieved a black plastic box with two tiny silver levers on the top.

The brilliant detective began counting down from ten in his head. He set the box on his desk in front of his laptop, and stood up a silver rod that had been laid flush in the back.

Loraine watched as Bone carefully extended the telescoping antenna. The complete scheme of Bone's plan became instantly clear.

Captain St. John set the coffee mug on his desk pad and the two donuts beside it. He licked a smudge of chocolate glaze off his index finger and thumb and took a seat.

Two, one. The silent countdown ended. Bone flipped the two control levers to *drive* and *full throttle* simultaneously.

Down the hall, the captain felt something grabbing at his ankles and making a low growling sound. He reacted instantly by slamming the chair back against the office wall, trying to get away.

"Son of a…"

He drew his Glock as he yanked up the desk to get eyes on the attacking creature.

David St. John wasn't sure what kind of animal it was, but the inactive Marine didn't take time to check. He triple tapped it at close range—the sound of rapid gunfire echoed up and down the halls of the normally placid police station.

St. John was still panting as the desk toppled over, sending his coffee and donuts to the carpet. The noise and motion of the RC car ceased as the scent of acid gunsmoke filled the small office.

Bone slammed the antenna down and glanced at Loraine. "Boogie time."

He picked up the remote control in one hand and grabbed his silverbelly Stetson from the hat rack on the wall with the other and headed for the door.

Loraine sat frozen for a second, stunned by the outcome of the prank.

Bone stopped at the door and looked back. "Comin'?"

She nodded and grabbed her purse.

Moomer stuck his head out of the break room. "What's goin' on?"

Bone looked over his shoulder as he passed. "Think the Cap'n was cleaning his sidearm."
"Huh?"

St. John stared at the creature he had killed. Then he saw the two front wheels of the model Hummer sticking out from under the raccoon fur.
"Damn you, Bone!"

§§§

CHAPTER TWO

COOKE COUNTY
RED RIVER VALLEY

"How do you want to set up, Miss Lisanne?"

Camera girl, Pat Reynolds, a cute twenty-six year old camera operator with light brown hair, leaned a tripod against the side of the white Ford news van for KTXP, Channel 14 parked on a logging road in Frog Bottom.

"You've been at this long as I have, Pat." The thirty something, very attractive brunette news reporter with her trademark captivating smile, Lisanne Miller, took her field wireless microphone out of its case. "What do you suggest?"

"Why don't I pick you up walking past the van with your intro and just as you clear, get the deputies searching in the background over your shoulder…Then you begin your report."

"Works for me, girl. Let's do it."

Pat shouldered the camera, instead of setting it on the tripod, and backed away from the van until she could see the sheriff deputies and detectives from Gainesville PD working their way through the brush, looking for clues, in the background.

They were as close to the crime scene as the Sheriff's Department would allow them.

Pat pointed a finger at Lisanne. "Rolling."

The experienced on-camera reporter began her walk. "This is Lisanne Miller with a live KTXP Channel 14 report from rural Cooke County. The body of a woman was discovered this morning by two local deer hunters in this wooded area behind me." Lisanne cleared the end of the van. "Cooke County Sheriff's department and detectives from the Gainesville police department are on the scene..."

Bone knelt beside the body, fifteen yards inside the woods.

Loraine stood beside Sheriff Brennan, a stocky fifty year old long time law officer. Gray hair showed beneath his light tan Stetson.

The body was a young mulatto woman, clad only in black thong panties, face down in the newly fallen crop of leaves. She had extremely long straightened hair. Her head was turned to the left and her eyes were open in death.

"'Preciate ya'll comin' out, Bone." He looked at Loraine, also. "Know this is out of your jurisdiction, but, you're the best crime scene investigator I know of..."

"Always glad to help out the Sheriff's department."

He pulled out a pair of double XL light purple latex gloves, blew into them to open them up, slipped them on, and began to examine the body.

Sheriff Brennan pushed his hat back from his forehead a little and leaned over with his hands on his knees. "So…what do you think?"

Bone didn't look up. "Judging from the amount of rigor mortis and the degree of decomposition…or lack of…My guess is she's been dead for about forty-eight hours." He looked up. "Wasn't killed here, though…just dumped."

Loraine also leaned in. "How do you know, Bone?"

He indicated the immediate area. "No sign of struggle, Pard, nothing disturbed…See the bruising on the sides of her neck? Consistent with manual strangulation…Also heavy petechial hemorrhage indicates suffocation.

"Patechial hemorrhage?"

Bone looked over at the sheriff. "Intradermal bleeding."

The sheriff shook his head. "Sorry I asked."

Bone continued his examination. "And the marks on her wrists? Looks like there was duct tape wrapped around them…removed post mortem. Bet Doc Fisk will find some adhesive residue when he does the autopsy."

The sheriff stood up. "This is the third murder with this MO in a three county area. Called in the Texas Rangers to coordinate the investigations."

"Well, big brother, looks like this is going to be a family affair."

Bone spun around at the sound of the voice and actually had to look up. "T-Bone!"

"T-Bone?" said Loraine and Sheriff Brennan together as they exchanged looks.

"Well, I'll be damned, little brother...Guess this is the only way to get you to come visit." Bone peeled his gloves off and they hugged, pounding each other on the back.

"Tiny, this is my partner, Senior Inspector Loraine Rodriguez...and you know the sheriff."

Tiny doffed his Texas Ranger silverbelly. "Pleasure, Loraine...How long ya'll been workin' together?"

"Almost a year now."

Tiny punched Bone on the shoulder, staggering him. "Hey, bro, new record."

"Bite me."

Loraine shook her head and looked up at the ranger, then at Bone. "This is the little brother you told me about?...Jesus, he's bigger than you."

25

"Yeah, he was a scrawny kid growing up, so I gave him part of my groceries."

"Think you over did it."

"He's two inches taller and…" He looked at Tiny. "…what? About fifteen pounds heavier?"

"Make it twenty if you're still 285."

"Yeah." Bone glanced at Loraine and the sheriff. "That's why the family calls him, 'T-Bone'…for Tiny Bone." He grinned. "Reminds me of that song by Don Ho, *Tiny Bubbles*…Or, well, better than Pork Chop…"

Tiny punched him again.

"Hate to break up the family reunion…"

"Yeah, sorry Sheriff, just catchin' up…" Tiny looked down at the body. "Looks like the same MO as the others…Think we got us a serial killer."

"Where were the other two murders?"

"Denton and Grayson counties, Loraine."

She nodded. "Puts Cooke County right smack in the middle.

"Let's bag her hands and turn her over, Bone. Just one more thing to match up for the MO."

Bone pulled out two more sets of the purple latex gloves and handed Tiny a pair—they slipped them on.

Bone bagged one hand with plastic bags, snapping a rubber band around the wrist, Tiny bagged the other. Then, they gently rolled her over to her back.

Loraine gasped, turned away and gagged.

Sheriff Brennan shook slightly like a rabbit had run across his grave. "Merciful God...Cut her breasts off..."

"Sweet Jesus," muttered Bone and looked at Tiny.

The big ranger nodded. "No question now."

NORTH TEXAS MEDICAL CENTER

Bone, Loraine, and Tiny strolled down the polished wide hallway to a set of double doors at the end on the right side.

Tiny pushed the near door open and nodded to Loraine.

"After you, M'lady."

"Thank you, kind sir." She looked back at Bone. "Not accustomed to such manners."

Bone raised both hands, palms up. "What?"

Loraine grinned. "You wouldn't understand."

They strode over to a stainless steel autopsy table where the County Medical Examiner, Doctor Burton Fisk stood. He was wearing his normal autopsy gown over his fluorescent green scrubbs, a brightly colored smock decorated with cartoon characters—this was his Disney day outfit.

The frumpy man, with thick glasses, always wore the same outfit consisting of a Hawaiian flowered shirt under his jacket and with black pants—except when he was performing an autopsy.

Bone stepped to the end of the table and proceeded to look at the victim's feet while Fisk gave his report.

"No question about it, she was not alive when her breasts were excised…almost no blood loss. Cause of death was asphyxiation by manual strangulation…not exsanguination…No sign that she was sexually assaulted."

Bone bent over for a closer look at her feet. "Let's get a scraping of the dirt on the soles of her feet, Doc…She was barefooted for some time…" He sniffed. "Getting an unusual smell. Kinda smells familiar…but can't place it right now…Sure is familiar, though."

Loraine shook her head. "Bone, only you would think to smell her feet."

He shrugged. "You never know...Tiny, were the other vics barefoot?"

He nodded. "Yep, just like this one...Only articles of clothing were panties...No one thought to scrape their feet though."

"I'll send Peach from forensics over to scrape her fingernails and feet and run 'em at her lab."

"Have the complete autopsy by tomorrow, Bone...Except for the tox screen, that is," said Fisk.

Bone pursed his lips. "Call me, Doc, I'm open nearly every day...laterbye."

He looked at Tiny and Loraine. "Well, children, lets's make like a cow patty and hit the trail."

"Only you, Bone."

Tiny grinned. "Oh, no, Loraine. I taught him that one."

"Dear God, help me." She led the way back down the hallway to the outside door of the hospital.

"Meet you at the station, T-Bone." Bone opened the door of his '71 Thing, got in, stuck his key in the ignition and started the engine.

Loraine stood at the passenger side with her arms folded across her ample bosom, tapping her foot on the asphalt.

Tiny waltzed over from his black sedan and opened her door.

Loraine cocked her head at Bone. "See." She looked back at T-Bone and winked.

GAINESVILLE PD
FORENSICS LAB

The tall brunette Georgia native, Peach Presley stood at the centrifuge as Bone walked in.

She looked up. "Well, looky here what the cat drug in...Hey, Bone, how are you?"

"Let me check..." He pulled the front of his shirt collar open and peered down inside. "...Yep, I'm good."

"Bone, that just makes my butt itch...I'm gonna quit askin'."

"Uh-huh,...say, Peach, while you're restin', need you to make a run over to Doc Fisk's and collect the fingernail scrapings and scrape the soles of a vic's feet...Be sure to get the toe jam."

"Oh, yuk, Bone. Kiss my go to hell. Bless your little pea-pickin' heart, you're sick, you know that?"

"What I heard...Let me know when you have an analysis, Pretty."

"Give me a couple of days...I'm busier than a moth in a mitten."

"Tomorrow...Laterbye.

"Bone, honey, you're like hemorrhoids...Pain in the butt when you come in an' a relief when you leave."

He giggled, left the lab, and headed in the direction of Captain St. John's office.

Loraine and Tiny Bone were sitting across from Captain St. John as Bone entered. They were watching Lisanne Miller doing a news report on the Captain's TV.

The perky news anchor was center screen. "Cooke County law enforcement officials are still mystified over the body of the young African-American woman found this morning. According to unofficial sources, the body was missing some parts and exhibited similar characteristics to two other female bodies found in Grayson and Denton counties. There is speculation that they may be the work of a serial killer…He's being called the North Texas Butcher…

The Captain turned from the TV. "Damn, how the hell did she find all that out? We'll have every woman in the area in a panic…Nobody talks about the MO, got it?…Everybody nod…So, what else do we have?…Bone?"

"It's definitely a serial killer, boss. Same MO on all three vics. Bound with duct tape, no sexual assault, breasts excised, strangled by someone with large hands…and all approximately the same age… mid-twenties to early thirties." He looked at his brother.

Tiny nodded. "All the vics were very attractive and apparently well endowed." He glanced at Loraine, his eyes drifted down to her ample bosom. "…No commonality as pertaining to race or hair color. Black, red and brown…"

"What did you look at me for?"

Tiny grinned. "Me?…Uh…Nothin'. Just, uh…wanted to see if you had anything to add."

She cut her eyes back at him. "Right...Now I got two to deal with," Loraine muttered. "Maybe the next one is set to be a blond..."

Bone, Loraine, and Tiny exchanged glances.

The captain looked at the three law officers individually for a long moment. "Well, let's see that there isn't a next one."

§§§

CHAPTER THREE

TIMBER CREEK SHOOTING RANGE

Bone turned off County Road 150 just past a single story wood frame home that sat forty yards off the road. He downshifted into second gear and hammered down on the Porche aircooled engine that he had shoehorned into his beloved VW. The lightweight '71 Thing responded like a dune buggy rail job and rocketed down the narrow lane leading to the pistol and rifle ranges used by the Gainesville PD.

He pulled in beside a long line of pickups trucks, SUVs, and even a few minivans owned by patrol officers with multiple young children.

Bone unzipped the outer pocket on an olive drab range bag and grabbed his custom fitted electronic ear plugs. He inserted one in each ear, and looking sixty yards to the north, he adjusted the volume to his liking as he eavesdropped on the conversations of some of his coworkers.

"Hey, Mone, get your butt down here. Everybody's waitin' on you," Moomer Martin called out with his characteristic speech impediment.

The big man glanced at his watch. It read 1:54. "What time does the 2:00 safety briefing start?"

"As soon as the weak link in the force shows his ugly face," Captain David St. John retorted.

Bone grinned, grabbed his range bag and strode quickly to the range house. He walked up to his much shorter boss. "Ain't still holding a grudge over that little ol' prank, are you, Cap'n?"

"Wouldn't think of it. Remember what we used to say in the Corps?"

"Never hold a grudge longer than it takes to get even?"

"No, nimrod...I was thinkin' more along the lines of 'paybacks are hell'."

Bone cracked up. "That, too...Gotta admit it was pretty realistic. Triple tapped it...I hear tell."

St. John eyes narrowed as he shook his head. "Don't push it, you big ox."

Chief Andy Anderson ambled out of the air conditioned classroom across the gravel road from the range shooting house. He was dressed identically to all the other LEOs—black tactical 511 pants, sunglasses, and a white cotton T shirt with huge block letters that spelled POLICE.

The Texas summer had held on for a full month past the official start of the fall season. It was still in the mid-eighties, but felt much hotter in the afternoon sun.

"All right, people, let's get this show on the road. Moomer, you have the roster made up for the first round of qualification?"

"You bet, Chief. Got it right here." He held up a twelve inch electronic notebook. "You and Captain St. John are in the first group."

The chief smiled as he picked up a pair of earmuffs off the peg board at the back of the non-air conditioned metal building.

Moomer grabbed a megaphone and called out the names of the rest of the first group. Bone and Loraine were also in it, along with Sergeant Richard Hung, Sergeant Rick Gore, rookie Juan Gomez, and Corporal Stella Johnson.

"Everybody make sure you have ear and eye protection," Moomer announced in his role of range master. "The course is fifty rounds. Move to your assigned shooting positions, place your weapon and ammunition on the table and stand by."

Each of the eight numbered positions had a tall three foot wide window from which the shooter could fire at a green silhouette turning target.

"Is the range ready?" Moomer stood behind the line of LEOs in the center where he could watch all eight. "Five rounds in ten seconds. Shooters may handle your weapons. Target is at three yards...Standby."

All the shooters picked up their loaded weapons. Loraine carried the only 1911 style pistol, a Kimber .45. She thumbed the safety off.

Moomer pressed a button on a remote control. A loud buzzer sounded, and every target turned to face the shooters.

A fusillade of rounds went down range, but, by the seven second mark, all the officers had completed their required five rounds.

When the time expired, the buzzer sounded again, turning the targets on edge.

"Five rounds in five seconds. Shooters may reload if needed...Shooters stand by."

Moomer watched Bone—the only qualifier using a wheel gun—dump the five humongous .500 S&W brass on the concrete pad and quickly slip a speed loader in.

Loraine dropped a partially full mag from her Kimber and slammed a full one home.

Bone gave him a *thumb's up* sign without looking back.

The rapid fire session sounded like a machine gun interspersed with five 105 Howitzer rounds. Bone's .500 had a muzzle brake that helped with recoil but made his hand cannon sound more like the real thing.

Loraine checked out her target. She was pleased with her inch and a half group. She glanced over at Bone's just before it turned.

"You have got to be kidding me."

What looked like a single, albeit slightly ragged hole, marked the exact dead center of his 10 ring.

Moomer hit the *travel* button on the remote control—the entire rack of eight frames moved back to the 10 yard marker. The final twenty shots would take place at 25 yards.

GAINESVILLE

A white Ford van pulled to the curb in a low rent neighborhood in the north part of the city. The houses were occupied mostly by Mexican immigrants, some legal, many illegal.

A large Anglo man got out of his seat stepped to the back and pulled a pair of rubber gloves from his pocket. He grabbed a big black plastic trash bag and started throwing some women's clothes, skirt, blouse, black bra cut in two between the D cups, and a pair of black high heels inside. When he finished, he looked carefully around the back of the van for anything he might have missed. Then he pulled the red built-in tie, knotted it, turned around, went back to the driver's seat, started up and pulled away from the curb.

The van pulled into the McDonald's drive and drove to the back. The driver stopped next to the dumpster and threw the trash bag inside. He then pulled over to the electronic order board and punched in an order for a Big Mac, fries, and a chocolate shake.

TIMBER CREEK SHOOTING RANGE

Moomer gave the order to clear and ground all weapons. Once that was done, he called out, "Shooters step back. The range is clear…Shooters, police your brass."

Bone picked up his empties and deposited them in plastic Ziplock bag for reloading.

"Ya'll can go down and retrieve your targets for scoring." Moomer called out to the next round of shooters, "Shooters, get your targets, go down range and set 'em up in the frame with your assigned number."

"How did you do, Pard?" Bone had a semi-smirk on his face as he walked alongside Loraine.

"Don't tell me that you didn't see that lone flyer."

"Saw it all right. Just wanted to know if you knew it when it happened."

"Of course I did. That monster wheel gun of yours made me flinch."

"Curse the luck…Not a bad group, all in all, Double D."

Rick Gore was happy with his three inch group, just slightly right of center in the ten ring. He walked back to the range house with Sergeant Hung. "How did you do?"

"I passed." There was no emotion shown by the night shift supervisor of Chinese descent. "Must learn to concentrate harder in order to reduce the mean impact pattern dispersal for a more favorable outcome, in respect to a higher score."

"Huh?"

St. John frowned at his target. "Two nines and an eight? What the hell is that? Must be losing it…"

Chief Anderson likewise was not impressed with his own showing. Two rounds barely clipped the green and another was outside the silhouette about two inches above the collar bone. He said nothing, as was his usual reaction to his shortcomings.

Inside the range house, Moomer tallied the scores, transferred the thumb drive to his department laptop and downloaded the information.

Stella looked at Bone's target with a little bit of jealousy.

He took a black magic marker and drew a symbol resembling a Milkbone dog biscuit—his personal signature—in the upper right hand corner.

"I wish I could learn to shoot like that."

He turned and looked down at her. "Really? Lemme see your target."

She showed it to him. Moomer had scored it a 225 out of 250. Three yard rounds had all been in the ten ring, but the farther out the target had been, the more the rounds drifted low and to the left.

"Think I see what's going on." Bone nodded knowingly.

"You can tell just by looking at the target?"

"Sure...Your Glock 17 is a little too big for your little hands...Puttin' the tip of the trigger finger on the side of the trigger...Makes the muzzle go left."

"You can tell that just by looking?"

Bone grinned. "Yes, Grasshopper...And the rounds in his belly button tell me you were jerking the trigger...Still have the factory trigger an' springs?"

She nodded.

"Figured...Get Rick to put a three and a half pound trigger spring in it...He's a huge Glock guy." He pointed at Sergeant Gore.

"Really?" Her face conveyed a slight bit of uncertainty.

"Child, have I ever jacked you around about anything serious?"

She shook her head.

"Go get your gun and range bag. We gotta skedaddle outta here, anyhow."

She did so, as Bone walked over to Rick. "Hey, buddy. You keep extra Glock trigger stuff in your armorer kits, don't you?"

"Sure…Thought you hated Glocks."

"Hate is perhaps too strong a word…They work great, just happen to have a strong disdain of their factory trigger compared to my Smith and Wesson."

"Gotcha…What'dya need?"

"Put a three and a half pound trigger pull on my little angel's Model 17 while we mosey over to the steel plate range. She needs some pointers." He took the semi auto from Stella and handed it to him.

"Piece of cake. Be inside the classroom…Got tables and A/C, you know."

§§§

CHAPTER FOUR

TIMBER CREEK SHOOTING RANGE

Bone grabbed his range bag and holstered his revolver. "Now for a little fun."

Loraine looked on with curiosity. "Hey, Pard. Mind if I tag along?"

"Not at all. Shouldn't take more than a couple of minutes."

It was Inspector Rodriguez's turn to raise her eyebrows.

Bone stood up three ten inch diameter, 3/8" thick steel plate targets, welded to heavy three foot long sections of two and 3/8" drill stem pipe that was, in turn, welded to old truck tire rims.

He took a can of spray paint left there on purpose, and refreshed the rusty gray steel discs to a uniform glossy white.

"Okay, Little Bit, gonna start out at fifteen yards, and shoot one round of the 275 grain Barnes at the one on the right. That first bullet impact will become your new target...Got it?"

"We're gonna shoot your 500?"

"No, don't be silly...*We* are not gonna shoot it...You are...I already know how." He smiled broadly.

"I don't know, I..."

Bone held up his hand. "Hush, hush...Stop right there. Not near as hard as those twelve years of competitive gymnastics you did, kiddo...Have I ever hurt you?"

Stella shook her head, her golden pony tail swayed back and forth in the afternoon sun.

"Not about to start now, either. Have to trust me, okay?" Bone unshucked the revolver, pulled a speed loader from his belt pouch and loaded five rounds.

"Lotsa folks love the so called Weaver stance. Me...not so much. I feel the same way about the FBI crouch. Anyway, drop your right foot back 'bout eighty to ninety degrees like this." He showed her.

"Now, your front foot should be thirty five to forty five degrees to the right of the target."

She moved her feet like Bone had shown. "Like this?"

"Exactly. Why did I do that, you ask?...'Cause it reduces my frontal target area, and allows me to drop my left arm against my rib cage...Provides support for my left hand. My right hand controls the weapon, but the left supports the weight of the weapon...Here, you try it." Bone handed the revolver over, muzzle down.

"But it's so heavy."

"Uh-huh...Gonna make you happy when you pull the trigger...trust me."

Stella fidgeted around until the position became more comfortable. "The one on the right…that what I'm shooting at?"

"Yes, ma'am. Thumb the hammer back when you're ready. Don't put your finger on the trigger until the sights are exactly where you want them…It ain't a Glock."

"Okay." Corporal Johnson took a couple of deep breaths, and let the last one out halfway. She found a sight alignment she liked and touched off the first round.

The 500 roared to life resulting in a rounding *clang* when the solid copper hollowpoint struck home.

A dark ring appeared around a newly formed dent in the plate where the paint was blasted away. The pistol bucked, but a smile came to the blond bombshell's face.

Loraine clapped and hollered, "Yay. You did it, girl!"

"Take your time…do it again." Bone was beaming.

Stella repeated the sequence until all five rounds were fired. Three went into the same hole and two were only a half inch apart. She was grinning like a possum eating persimmons.

"Good job, young'un. Hand me my baby...As they said on Monte Python, 'and now for something completely different'."

"It's amazing...didn't kick any more than my Dad's .44 Mag Super Blackhawk." She handed the weapon to him.

"Not with the light loads, at least. These are the 350s...You will feel a difference."

She locked eyes with her teacher.

"You can handle it...Let 'er rip."

Stella was still a little apprehensive when she touched off the first round. The impact topped the stand over, truck rim and all.

"Oh my God!" She stood with her mouth agape.

"Didn't see that coming did you? Take out the other two using double action...Strong steady pull on the trigger."

The petite blond took in two more deep breaths and stared at the remaining targets.

Loraine called out, "You got this!"

Stella raised the big revolver up and snapped off two aimed shots as quickly as she could. Both targets crashed to the ground.

"I did it! I did it!" She jumped up and down.

Bone held out his hand. "Don't pee your pants...Save some for the pumpkins."

"What? We're gonna shoot at pumpkins?"

She handed the revolver over to him carefully, as it was still loaded.

"Tomorrow...I forget you *are* a natural blond...Don't you know why they call the fall pistol qualification a pumpkin shoot?"

"Guess I didn't make the connection." She shrugged and grinned sheepishly.

"Never mind that...Girl, you are now an official member of Bone's 500 Badass Club." He held up a hand for a high five.

Stella took a swipe at his hand, but he raised it over ten feet, putting it out of her 5'3" range.

Loraine moved in to give her a big hug. "Proud of you...You done good." She glared at Bone. "Forget that jackalope. He just can't help himself."

The three gathered their gear and went into the classroom to find Rick putting the slide back in place on her Glock.

"Try it now, should be a lot nicer." He offered it to her.

Stella racked it and gave the trigger a test. "Wow. Lot's better…What do I owe you?"

"Nothin'…worth it just to see you smile."

"Maybe I can make dinner for you some time."

"Sounds like a deal." He grinned.

GAINESVILLE, TEXAS
GOVERNOR'S LOUNGE

The local bar was loaded with cops. Loraine, Stella, Wanda Stanton, Juan Gomez, St. John, Peach, and Tiny Bone were seated around a large round table, chatting, listing to Ginny Mac on stage and drinking beer.

Sheriff Brennan was dancing with the proprietor, Vertis Jolley, a fifty year old attractive woman with premature gray hair.

Ginny was singing her original song, *Dancin' On The A*.

She finished it to everyone in the club's rousing applause and some whistles.

Ginny nodded her appreciation. "Thank you…Gonna take a short pause for the cause…Back in a few."

She stepped off the stage and walked over to the cop's table. Sheriff Brennan was just taking his seat.

Stella glanced up as Tiny pulled out a chair for Ginny. "Wow, girl, you are hot tonight...Need a beer?"

The good looking songstress with long raven tresses, grinned. "You buyin', Stella?"

"At least the first one."

"Gotta start somewhere," responded Ginny.

Wanda, a patrol officer, asked, "Hey, Loraine, where's Bone?"

"Said he had some errands to run...Should be here about..." She looked at her watch. "...now."

The front door opened, Bone stepped inside and hung his hat on the tree by the door. He was still wearing his S&W 500 on his belt.

Vertis stepped up to the big man. "Evenin' Bone."

He grinned at her. "Vertis...Looks like the place is still standing."

"Yeah, so far...'Course, the night's young yet." She looked at his pistol. "How many times are we going to have this discussion?"

"What discussion?"

Vertis frowned. "Your gun...I've asked you umpteen times not to wear a loaded gun in my club."

"Vertis...I'm a cop."

"Don't care...Creates a bad image in my club."

Bone rolled his gold-flecked brown eyes, turned, pushed the door back open, drew his weapon, stuck it out the door, pointed it to the sky and fired all five rounds."

The roar of the 'worlds largest handgun' was deafening, even inside the club. He put the weapon back into his holster and closed the door.

"Not loaded now."

Vertis shook her head. "Don't you get tired of doin' that?"

He shook his head. "Not as long as they keep makin' awnings."

She turned and walked back to the bar, muttering, "Why me, Lord."

Bone smiled, showing his dazzling white teeth and walked toward the table where Loraine and the others were sitting.

Stella looked up as he pulled out a chair. "Bone do you just like buyin' awnings?"

He looked down at her. "One of life's little pleasures, Stella."

Captain St. John took a sip of his Corona long neck. "Better be glad the mayor's not around."

Everyone voiced greetings as he sat down.

"It's past his bed time." Bone looked at the pyramid of long necks. "See ya'll started without me."

Loraine finished off her Michelob Ultra. "Just warmin' up."

"Not me, I'm done, got duty shift at midnight. I'm outta here." Wanda got up, threw some bills on the table. "This oughta cover my ice tea."

Stella also got up and pitched a twenty on the table. "I'm gone too, hate to leave such a rockin' party, but, I gotta pick up some groceries before the stores close."

"See you in the morning, Stella," said her patrol partner, Gomez.

"Don't be late."

"You keeddin'? Still healin' from being late the last time."

"That was just a sample." She grabbed her purse and walked toward the door.

Sheriff Brennan watched her sashay to the front door, her long pony tail swayed to the rhythm of her shapely hips. "There goes a good cop in the makin'…Wish I'd have found her first."

"Yeah, a few years under her belt, she'll be a Ranger candidate…Wanda's no slouch either."

St. John nodded at Tiny. "You'll have to fight me for either one of 'em."

Stella drove into the driveway of her small rented house on Pecan Street. She got out of her small Honda SUV, walked around to the hatch and pressed the lever to open it. It lifted up, she grabbed three plastic bags of groceries, set them on the ground, closed the lid, picked them up, and headed to the small house.

Across the street under the shadow of a large white oak tree, a large man in a white Ford panel van watched Stella until she entered the house. When the lights came on, he started the vehicle, pulled away from the curb, and turned his lights on when he was almost a block away.

§§§

CHAPTER FIVE

COOKE COUNTY
FM 678

The blacked-out late model Ford Mustang braked hard for the exit off of westbound Texas Highway 82. It had been clocking over a hundred—in a sixty five mile per hour zone. The custom low back pressure mufflers rumbled as the driver downshifted to fourth gear, then all the way to second for the hard right-hand turn at the junction with Farm to Market 678.

The driver was focused on the slight drift and the oncoming gold pickup in the southbound lane on FM 678 and didn't see the scrap piece of 1"x4" door trim lying in the right lane.

She didn't feel too much of a bump and the finishing nail wasn't very large—just barely long enough to make it through the tire's plies.

The driver ran though the gears, accelerating to 115 on the rural road and exhilarating at the car's taut handling on the curves and hills.

Three miles north, the road dropped into a deep valley. The Mustang tach climbed to almost three thousand RPM before a dashboard caution light came on and the warning beep sounded.

"Dammit! Low tire pressure? What's up with that? These are brand new Pirellis."

The driver braked, downshifted and brought the sports car to a halt near the bottom of the valley. The two lane road had a paved shoulder, allowing the driver to pull over and turn off the ignition.

Muttering to herself, the statuesque strawberry blonde checked the rearview mirror, opened the door and stepped out. She took one look at the left front tire and knew the pressure sensor was not lying.

"What a way to screw up a perfect day."

She glanced at her highly polished French manicured nails and decided against trying to change the tire herself. "At least I bought roadside assistance...Money well spent." She leaned over inside the car and retrieved her cell phone.

She opened the screen and scrolled through her contacts. "Here we go...AAA. Earn your money, people." She tapped the green telephone icon.

The next page really ticked her off. "No Service? What do you mean No Service?"

Sure enough, there were no bars at the top of the screen.

A white Ford van came down the hill headed in the same direction. The driver, a large Anglo man, slowed down and checked out the well-endowed woman standing next to a black Mustang.

Her gray yoga pants were all but sprayed on and her coral tank top left absolutely nothing to the imagination.

He braked and pulled over on the shoulder a couple of car lengths ahead of her.

"Thank God for southern gentlemen," she muttered.

The driver of the van slipped a pair of disposable plastic gloves into a thigh pocket on his cargo pants. A leather lead-filled sap went into his right back pocket as he exited the van. He smiled and headed her way.

She looked at the large man. "God, he's big enough to play for the Cowboys."

Part of her was alarmed by the remoteness of the rural place and his size, but he smiled as he called out, "Need some help, Ma'am?"

"Yeah, got a stinkin' flat." She pointed at her right front tire.

The man was only five feet from her when he saw a black and white cruiser from the Texas Highway Patrol coming down the hill from the south.

"Your lucky day, Miss. Here comes the cavalry to the rescue."

The highway patrolman slowed, pulled over behind her, and turned on his rollers.

The big man pointed to the trooper. "He'll take good care of you. Have a great day, hear?" He turned around, climbed into his van and drove off as the state trooper stepped out of his car.

TIMBER CREEK SHOOTING RANGE

The fall sun hovered a little above the tree tops. The days were getting shorter, but it was still light enough at 5PM for shooting.

Inside the classroom, the Chief held the *Qualification complete* report from Moomer. "Okay, people good report, everyone qualified yesterday…Time to break out the Road and Bridge Kit."

"Now you're talking." Bone held the door open for the others.

All sixteen qualifiers, plus the range master gathered outside the classroom.

Chief Anderson made a brief speech, "Congratulations on another successful quarterly handgun qualification course. I want to especially thank Sergeant Richard Hung for doing such a fine job acquiring the pumpkins for this shoot. Let's give him a round of applause."

A few of the assembled clapped politely. Bone was not one of them.

"And now, without further adieu, I hereby declare this meeting of the Road and Bridge Club in session…Beer time!"

The group hollered and clapped with gusto. Moomer dropped the tailgate of his Ford 350 pickup, exposing a somewhat weather-beaten sixty quart Igloo cooler with the words *ROAD AND BRIDGE CLUB* hand painted in black letters.

He jumped up on the tail gate, lifted the lid and began passing out longnecks, still coated with shaved ice.

Everybody seemed to get their favorite. The captain preferred Corona, Stella liked Bud Light, Loraine latched on to a Michelob Ultra, and Bone always insisted on Shiner Bock.

After everyone had at least two brews, it was time to head to the lower range for the *pièce de résistance*—the ritual massacre of defenseless pumpkins—especially the ones filled with Tannerite. Excitement was building.

Moomer had moved the A frame from the upper pistol range to the lower range. A single ten pound pumpkin was suspended by a wire near one end of the frame. He had rigged up an electronic relay to release the large gourd once the two rookie cops were at the firing line.

Juan Gomez was a little nervous.

Stella, his training partner for his first three months called out, "You can do it, Julio!"

He turned around and shot her a look, and then grinned. "It's still Juan."

"Whatever," she replied, keeping their ongoing inside joke alive.

Sandra Parker, the other rookie, was only four weeks out of the academy. She acted more confident, relying on the large capacity twenty-one round mag of her new Sig 320.

"Ya'll have thirty seconds once the horn sounds. Shooters ready...Stand by..." Moomer triggered the release, and almost immediately, pressed the button on a boat horn.

The large orange globe swung through its arc like a giant pendulum. Both rookies drew their weapons and unleashed a small war. Nine millimeter rounds peppered the hillside, but did not touch their intended moving target.

The crowd of seasoned cops roared with laughter. They had all been humiliated by the same challenge.

Juan reloaded and dumped another fifteen rounder at the still moving target.

Sandra fumbled with her reloading, frustrated by her lack of success. She got her lone backup mag inserted in the well and blasted away. Again no hits.

Both rookies holstered their empty weapons as the pumpkin's arc became smaller and smaller. Juan looked at Sandra and shrugged. She simply shook her head.

"I am so happy that you guys qualified earlier. You probably didn't bring enough ammo to finish the course now." Gore grinned.

"All right, smart guy. Let's see you do it. Moomer, set it up again." The Chief crossed his arms.

"You got it, boss." Moomer stepped forward as the two rookies wandered back somewhat dispirited.

With the release attached to the small steel plate glued to the pumpkin, Moomer retreated back to the twenty-five yard range. "Show 'em what the TAC team can do," he whispered to Rick.

Gore inserted a mag filled with jacketed hollowpoints into his Glock. He stood facing the A frame with both hands held up head high in the competition ready stance.

"Shooter ready...Stand by..." Moomer released the target and sounded the horn.

Gore drew quickly and followed the pumpkin until it paused for a split second at the top of its first swing. He double tapped it, knocking chunks of orange and white pith out the backside.

He repeated the process at the apex of the backswing and then ventilated the moving pumpkin rapid fire until his slide locked back. As the crowd roared its approval, he turned around and, in a theatrical twist, Rick blew the last bit of gunsmoke from the pistol's muzzle.

"Bravo," Bone hollered. "Hope you rookies were takin' notes."

"Holy crap," Juan whispered to Sandra. "Did you see that?"

"Uh huh. Know who I want to call for backup."

A pickup truck load of punkin's, as Bone called 'em, was unloaded and set out on the hillside backstop.

Moomer brought out a 5.56 M4 carbine with iron sights. "Who wants to be the first to blow up some Tannerite?"

Captain St. John stepped forward. "Just like the one I had in the Corps." He took control of the weapon and aimed carefully. The rifle fired, but nothing happened down range save a bit of dust kicked up behind the target.

"You sure you put some boom boom powder in that one?" St. John was clearly disappointed.

"'Course I did. Little bitty canister, aim a bit lower." Moomer held up one of the ¼ pound plastic bottles. It was only three inches around and three inches tall.

"Alrighty then. Here goes nothin'."

At his second shot, aimed just above the bottom of the target, the pumpkin exploded with a tremendous roar that could be heard a mile away. The vegetable turned into a starburst of tiny orange and white fragments. The crowd cheered.

Forty minutes later, the hillside was littered with chunks of the decimated fall pumpkins.

Moomer called over to Rick. "Gimme a hand here. It's the last of the Mohicans."

Gore eased over to the truck bed and looked inside. "Leapin' lizards...How much does that thing weigh?"

"Dunno. Ain't got a scale, but bet it's close to a hundred."

They struggled to get it off the tail gate.

Rick grinned. "Ain't got any handles, either."

Bone noted their frustration. He moved in. "Okay, kiddies. Step aside...Looks like a job for Mighty Bone...Here I come to save the day..."

"Go for it Conan. Show the mortals how its done." Rick crossed his arms.

The big man reached over the huge pumpkin with his left hand and slid it easily onto his right palm. He lifted it up as if it was a cup of coffee. "Where do you want this, Moomer?"

"'Bout fifty yards over there." He pointed in front of the hanging target frame.

Gore stood slack jawed for a second before he was able to softly mutter, "Holy crap."

Moomer escorted Bone to the selected site. "Set her down easy, Mone. Got three pounds of Tannerite in there."

Bone eased it down and adjusted it slightly to present the prettiest side to the shooter.

Moomer retrieved his megaphone for the last announcement. "Folks, this will conclude the last of the official Pumpkin Shoot. In honor of my able assistant, and the man who came up with the idea of blowing up pumpkins years ago...I ask Detective Darrell Bone to take the last shot."

Loraine showed her surprise. "You never told me you came up with this."

"Man's gotta have some secrets." He turned to the crowd. "Folks. I am truly honored...can't say I'm humbled, cause that would be a lie."

Everyone laughed.

"Anyway, I'd like to share this honor with Corporal Stella Johnson. Girl shows grit and determination, and impressed me with my big stick, Theodore, here." He patted his huge sidearm. "Get over here, Stella."

She reluctantly worked her way through the crowd. "Nothing like putting me on the spot, huh?"

He shook his head. "I got faith. You could use some, Little Bit." He drew the weapon and handed it to her.

She turned to face the target, and then moved into the stance Bone taught her.

Chief Anderson eased into a position beside her. *This I gotta see. No way is this little slip of a girl's gonna handle that hand cannon.*

The crowd was silent as they watched her concentrate on the front sight. She cocked the hammer back in single action and let out some of her breath.

When the hammer fell, the 500 became a fire breathing dragon once more. In a split second the huge pumpkin ceased to exist.

Three pounds of explosive made a huge fireball, a deafening roar, and sent fragments out 100 yards.

Almost as if in slow motion, Stella watched a jagged three inch chunk fly almost directly at her. She was mesmerized as the pumpkin rind did not rotate or spin at all. It got bigger and bigger as it rocketed past her—directly into the Chief's crotch.

Anderson reacted by grabbing at his injured privates. He slammed his knees together and dropped to the ground, bent over in pain—he looked up at an astonished Stella.

The Chief crossed his eyes, mouthed the word, "Ow," and toppled slowly to the turf sideways.

§§§

CHAPTER SIX

GAINESVILLE PD
INSPECTOR'S UNIT

Bone, Loraine, and Tiny pulled their chairs in front of the fifty inch monitor on the side wall so they could view close-ups of the evidentiary information and the reports for the three murders, looking for commonalties.

Loraine was operating the remote and had pulled up autopsy photos of the victims.

"Zoom in on the necks of all three vics and give us a side by side view, Pard."

She manipulated the buttons and the screen came to life with the photos.

"The bruising on the sides of the necks, plus the crushed laryngeal prominence, Adam's apple, indicates to me that the perp is very strong with large hands." Bone pointed to the three close-up pictures of the three girl's necks.

"You can even make out the individual fingers on the sides…You're right, Bone, big hands," added Loraine. "And no prints."

"Used gloves, I'm sure," said Bone. "He's no dummy…Knows we can pull prints from skin with today's technology."

Tiny nodded as he studied the photographs. "Uh-huh…Did Doc Fisk give an opinion if the girls were alive when they were strangled?…Or was it COD?"

Bone shook his head. "COD and nope, just said they weren't alive when their breasts were excised."

"That's one good thing," said Loraine.

"Any chance of pulling DNA?"

"Not from the perp, T-Bone…According to the reports, the vics were all killed someplace else, and then dumped in some rural area," added Bone.

"Zoom in on the breast area, Loraine." Tiny leaned forward in his chair. "Tighter right on the edge of the incision."

Loraine keyed the remote and the red area where the breasts once were filled the monitor's screen.

Tiny nodded again. "Uh-huh, no question about it."

"What?" asked Loraine.

Bone jumped in before Tiny could answer. "Whoever did this knew something about surgery."

"And you can tell how?"

Bone glanced at his partner. "The boobs weren't hacked off with any old knife or butcher's cleaver…" He pointed to the screen again. "That cut is most likely by some kind of razor and is almost perfect."

"So, you're saying a doctor did this?"

T-Bone shook his head. "Not necessarily, Loraine, anyone with any knowledge of anatomy, training or practice in cutting flesh would be on the list...besides doctors, you got veterinarians, chefs, nurses, even butchers or, goin' out on a limb...a sculptor who works with clay maybe."

"Well, that cuts the list down to a few thousand in the three county area." Bone leaned back in his chair and gazed at the ceiling.

"He's done a brown haired woman, a white redhead and now an African American...next could well be a blond."

Tiny glanced at Loraine. "Or could be a well-endowed Hispanic with sable hair..."

"Humpf...Wish he'd try."

"Loraine is a seventh degree black belt Kung Fu, T-Bone...Can turn you every which way but loose."

Tiny looked at her with appreciative eyes. "Ooo, nice."

Bone's cell phone rang with the William Tell Overture. "Bone...whatcha got, Peach?"

"Got a minute?"

"For you, anytime."

"Need you to come down to the lab."

"Got something?"

"Could say."

"Be right down."

Bone hit the off button on his Galaxy 7 and slipped it back in his shirt pocket.

"Peach says to come down to her lab…Must have something interesting."

They got to their feet, headed out the door and down the hall to the Forensics Lab.

Bone pushed the door open.

Peach was standing over at the center island and was looking through her microscope at a slide. She keyed her controls and the image appeared on a twenty-five inch monitor mounted above the island.

There were various types of particles on the screen. She moved the slide around and fiddled with the focus knob.

Peach turned to the trio and rubbed her eyes. "Hey, Bone, Loraine…What is this? They clonin' you now?"

"My baby brother, Tiny…He's a Texas Ranger." He turned to him. "This is Peach Presley, our Forensics tech. Got more degrees than Carter's got liver pills." He looked back at Peach. "We call him…"

She grinned showing her even white teeth and held up her hand. "Betcha a nickel ya'll call him T-Bone."

Tiny wrinkled his brow. "How…"

"Honey, I was born at night, but not last night…What I'd call him…Tiny an' Bone…T-Bone…duh." She grinned again and looked him up and down. "You're a whole lot cuter'n Bone…'Course that ain't sayin' a whole lot."

Tiny smiled back. "Not sure how to take that, Peach, but I'll jump out an' take it as a compliment."

"Close enough for government work…I finished the analysis of the fingernail scrapin's, no skin cells…also did the scrapin' from the vic's feet…includin' the toe jam."

Bone arched his eyebrows. "And?"

Peach pointed at her monitor. "Grain dust an' molasses…Most of the grain is milo, some wheat bran, rye, corn, oats and traces of S+NaCl.

"S+NaCl?" Loraine looked puzzled.

Salt, sugar pie, more particularly…livestock salt."

"What makes livestock salt different?" asked Tiny.

"Has sulfur in it."

"Feed, hah...That's what I was smelling." He looked over at Loraine. "Ever been in a feed store?"

She shook her head. "Can't say that I have."

Bone glanced back at Tiny. "We have...growing up."

"Hauled many a bag out to the farm for the horses, chickens, an' cows." Tiny grinned. "Used to love to go in the warehouse behind the store, layin' back on top of a pallet of sweetfeed for a hour just takin' in the smells...Nothin' smells like a feed store."

"No wonder I was always havin' to load the feed into the pickup...Couldn't figure out where you were."

Tiny shrugged. "Mama didn't raise no fool...got a brother."

Bone slugged his shoulder.

"I like him...he's precious." Peach looked up at Tiny. "Bless your heart, buttercup, we need to go have a glass of ice tea an' visit sometimes."

"Works for me." He grinned again.

"All right, ya'll stroke each other some other time, we got work to do...gotta find this house ape before he gets number four."

Bone looked at Tiny. "Just so you know, brother, Peach can charm the dew right off the honeysuckle."

Peach put her fists on her shapely hips. "Don't you go to butterin' my biscuit, Bone...I'll jerk you baldheaded."

Bone giggled and turned to Tiny. "And she will, too."

Corporal Wanda Stanton drove to the station and parked in the employee lot. She glanced the digital display on the dashboard. "11:35...still have ten minutes to check the B-board and potty."

She was already dressed for duty, except for her shoulder length brown hair that was still hanging down. The thirty year old single cop locked her Toyota Camry and headed into the station.

Once inside, Wanda scanned the break room bulletin board for things of interest. Finding only stale donuts and nothing new since her last shift, she turned and was walking toward the ladies room when she passed rookie Sandra Parker coming in.

"How was your day?"

Sandra shook her head. "Couldn't sleep worth beans…these graveyard shifts are kickin' my behind."

Wanda chuckled and nodded her agreement. "Heard that. Takes me about two weeks to get adjusted to the new schedule, four weeks of relative normal sleep and then we rotate again. Shift is a four letter word."

"Maybe things will be quiet tonight. We can always hope."

Officer Stanton grinned. "Don't bet the farm on it."

Inside the ladies room, she took care of her business and washed her hands. She dug in her front pocket, retrieved an elastic light brown scrunchy, slipped it over her right thumb and index finger.

Looking in the mirror, she pulled her hair back into a medium length pony tail and snugged the hair band in place.

Wanda grabbed her black GPD ball cap from her locker and headed to the briefing room. She slipped into a chair beside her rookie partner, Juan Gomez. He had graduated from the training academy in Sherman three months earlier and was almost off his *dual officer only* status. His first cycle was with Stella.

"Hey, girl...sup?"

"Just the usual. Moon's gettin' full."

"Noticed. Is it true what they say about them?"

"Most certainly...can be rather...eventful at times. I expect Sergeant Hung to go into it in painfully excruciating detail." She leaned closer. "Boy was vaccinated with a phonograph needle."

"Huh? What's that?"

Wanda just stared at him as four other officers filed in and took their seats.

Sergeant Richard Hung entered at exactly 23:45 hours on the digital clock behind the podium. He couldn't shoot very well and was barely able to pass the annual PT test, but he was a stickler on two things—Paperwork and Punctuality. He had a Meerschaum pipe clenched in his teeth.

He eyeballed the six officers closely before he removed the pipe and set it down carefully on the podium. It didn't seem to matter that the Chief had banned tobacco use entirely in the station house. Hung never planned to smoke it, anyway. It seems that Detective Bone had convinced the up-and-coming police officer that a pipe would somehow make him look more distinguished.

"Welcome to the October 29th briefing for the third shift. We shall begin with roll call. Please call out your last name and badge number."

The officers exchanged glances. Wanda had to cover her mouth with her hand to keep from bursting out laughing.

Once the last one had reported, Hung made the obligatory entry into his official tablet and pressed *Enter*.

"Very well. My prepared comments for tonight are as follows..." He read the three pages of notes pertaining to his words of wisdom regarding as he put it, "...scientifically observed correlations between lunar phase and antisocial, aberrant behavioral deviations."

His delivery was in a flat monotone, and he never once made eye contact with the other officers. Almost as an afterthought, he added a few sentences about a probable serial killer in the local area.

Wanda and Juan glanced at each other.

Hung ended his briefing as always. "Be safe, Protect and serve." He picked up his pipe, stuck it in his mouth and left the room.

Juan leaned in to his partner. "Is he always this boring?"

She laughed. "'Course not...Sometimes he's a lot worse."

The radio crackled to life at 12:30 AM. "Unit 27, dispatch."

Juan reached for the microphone. "Unit 27...Go ahead, Lauri."

The twenty year old Police Science student at the local North Central Texas College called back, "See the woman at the address on your screen. Reports of a nude man at the Glenwood Apartments."

Wanda nodded. "Got it."

"Unit 27 en route. ETA two minutes, over."

"Dispatch roger."

Juan tapped on the touch screen. The contact information had a name and apartment number.

Once he touched the screen, her driver license was cross referenced and displayed.

"Tammy Joe Tyler...Say's here she's an eighty-four year old Caucasian livin' in apartment 203...Ever had contact with her before?"

The eight year brunette veteran nodded. "Just when I thought the night was gonna be a cakewalk."

Wanda turned right off Fair Avenue and accelerated down East Hwy 82. Three blocks later, she turned left off the nearly deserted four lane highway into a parking lot for multiple two story buildings. She found an empty spot near the stairwell closest to the complainant. The entire place was rent subsidized Section 8 housing. All the cops in the department were intimately familiar with it.

Turning off the cruiser, Wanda gave a fake smile to Juan. "Time to *protect and serve*, amigo."

Both officers stepped out and Wanda motioned for him to follow her.

At the top of the stairs, she turned right without even looking at the apartment numbers. Two doors down, she rapped on the tarnished brass knocker and waited.

A little old woman, barely standing five feet tall opened the door wearing a badly faded cotton housecoat and fluffy pink slippers. "Took you long enough...He's still naked."

"Ms Tyler, I'm Corporal Wanda Stanton, and this is Officer Juan Gomez."

"Yeah, you came here before when they were having that party with god awful music...Like to have deafened me."

"Yes Ma'am. I remember. Where is this nude man you saw?"

"Across the way...I saw him out of my bathroom window. I'll show you."

She slowly turned around and shuffled across the living room and down the hall. Both officers followed her.

"Can you describe the man?"

She looked over her shoulder at Gomez. "Of course, dummy. He's butt nekkid as a jaybird. His weenie is hanging down halfway to his knees. Man has no sense of decency whatsoever."

Wanda choked back a laugh. It almost sounded like a cough. Juan snorted.

She led them into a modest bath set between the two tiny bedrooms. It had a shower and a short vanity with a gloss white commode set across from an open linen storage shelf. A small 1'x2' window was on the north facing wall between the shelf and the toilet.

Tammy Joe pointed at the window. "You can see for yourself right through there."

Wanda looked at Juan. "You can do the honors."

He stepped closer and peered out the window. Most of the other apartments were black that time of night. One had a flickering blue light from a movie on a flat screen TV.

It was ninety feet across the apartment complex courtyard. Juan could barely make out the man's head and part of his chest as he reclined propped up on two large pillows.

He turned to face the retired librarian. "Ma'am, I can't see anything out of the ordinary from here."

She shook her head in disgust. "Of course not! You have to stand up on the toilet…It helps if you use these." Tammy Joe pulled a small pair of 7x35 binoculars from a pocket in her housecoat.

§§§

CHAPTER SEVEN

BONE RANCH

"Never in my wildest dreams did I think I'd own a section of land, house, cattle, and a '30 Cord Coupe with less than three thousand miles on it, not to say anything about all that gold and diamonds Lucy left me."

Lucy was the diminutive stranded Anunnaki from the crashed alien ship in 1898 who was waiting on rescue from her people. Her people were known throughout the world for thousands of years as 'the grays', but in reality people were seeing them in their spacesuits as they looked just like us, only smaller—or it could be said we looked like them, only larger.

Bone's godfather, Padrino, a seventy year old retired Master Gunnery Sergeant from the Marine Corps and a reluctant Shaman sat in a rocking chair next to Bone's.

"Everything has a purpose, Bone. I fear she would not have survived had you not interceded for her with that unscrupulous energy company so her people could rescue her."

"I know, but still…"

"Don't mean to use old clichés, but don't look a gift horse in the mouth. As in all things…Look at nothing, my son, but see everything."

Bone reached down and petted Tyrin's head, Lucy's muscular blond and white pit bull that came along with the ranch and other things.

"Suppose you're right, Padrino.

Bone got to his feet. "Got some thick-cut top sirloin. Thinkin' about Chinese stir fry. You man enough to handle Szechwan?"

Padrino gave him a hard look. "You can't make it too hot for a salty 'Nam vet like me."

"Sounds like a challenge." A grin spread across his face.

GAINESVILLE

"Is it always this quiet on the night before Halloween?" Officer Parker scanned the houses in the neighborhood as they drove slowly down Dixon Street.

Newman, twenty-eight with his blond hair in a white-sidewall crewcut, glanced over at his cute rookie partner with short light brown hair who was only in her fourth week out of the academy. "Sometimes yes…sometimes no. Can be quiet as a graveyard…no pun intended, and then all hell can break loose…Just got to be ready."

Patrol officers, Corporal Joel Newman and rookie Sandra Parker, were well into the midnight or graveyard shift.

"It's after two…usually quiet this time of night anyway. Drunks are either passed out or already home." Newman chuckled. "Guess we better make a loop through Leonard Park…case there's some parkers playin' grab ass or some aforementioned drunks that couldn't make it home."

"Couldn't make it home?"

"Yeah, you know, mama'll peel their head they come in drunk, so they sleep it off sometimes in the pavilion."

"I don't know that I'll ever get married. My husband ever went out and got drunk without me, I'd do more than peel his head."

Newman chuckled again. "Talk's cheap."

The black and gold unit pulled into the entrance to the large well-kept park that included an Olympic-sized city pool, a large pavilion, and the Frank Buck Zoo. The park bordered the Elm Fork of the Trinity River.

They drove very slowly past the green metal roofed pavilion, Sandra flashed the spotlight on the passenger side through the middle of the facility.

"Hold it…got somethin'."

Newman braked the unit.

"All right kid, go roust him out. Flash light in your left hand, right on your taser…Be nice, but don't take no gaff. Got it?"

She nodded, got out and walked to the pavilion and climbed the short concrete steps. A drunk was asleep on top of one of the picnic tables that were set under the roof.

"Okay, wake up." She kicked the crossed table leg, shaking the table. "Hey, you…wake up."

"Huh…What…I'm up honey, I'm up." The man blinked his eyes and set up. "Who…"

"Officer Parker…Can't sleep here. Go home…Can you drive?"

He shook his head to clear it and stepped down to the concrete floor. "Got here, didn't I?"

"Don't get smart, you know what I mean." She shined her light on a concrete section line. "Walk that line with your arms out to the side."

"Frontwise or backwise?"

"Just do it."

He looked down at the crack and tiptoed like a ballerina walking a tightrope.

"You a dancer?"

"Awe, no…Just drunk…Hey!" He grinned and pointed at her.

Sandra pointed back. "Gotcha." She shook her head and grinned. "Anybody you can call to come pick you up?"

"Naw, jest my old lady...an' she'll kill me...Let me stay here an' sleep it off...please...purty please with sugar on it?" He dropped to his knees and put his hand together in supplication. "Please...Ain't gonna bother nobody...honest Injun."

Sandra sighed. "Okay, but you be gone from here at sunup, before the park opens...Hear me?"

"Oh, thank you, thank you." He reached out to hug her.

She backed up. "Uh-uh...I'll hurt you...Now get back on that table an' do what I told you."

"Yes, Ma'am, I can do that. Yes, Ma'am, you bet."

He crawled back on the table, laid down, folded both hands under the side of his face and was snoring before Parker walked down the steps. She got back in the patrol car.

"You learn quick, kid." Joel smiled, put the unit in gear and pulled on down the tree shrouded lane in the park.

They rounded the curve at the south end of the park in front of the zoo. Joel and Sandra could plainly hear the animals at the west side of the zoo raising all sorts of hell. The lions were roaring, the hyenas laughing, and some of the exotic antelopes were running back and forth.

"What the sam hill…" Newman stopped the unit.

They both got out with their flashlights.

"This can't be right." Parker shined her light into the fenced-off animal compound. "They shouldn't be agitated this time of night."

She and Newman systematically searched the area with their lights inside the enclosure.

"Nothin'." Parker glanced over at her partner.

"Gotta be somethin' outside that's got 'em stirred up."

The officers walked toward the embankment that led down to Elm Fork Creek, plying their powerful lights along the bank and into the water.

"What's that?" Parker aimed her flashlight at something light colored that bounced back at her.

"Oh, God, oh God." She looked at Joel as he walked up beside her.

"What?"

She flashed her light back down the slope of the levee, almost six feet from the edge of the creek.

"Oh, Jesus…a body." Newman grabbed the mic on his shoulder. "Lauri, this is unit 22.

"Dispatch…Go ahead 22."

"Got a 187 at Leonard Park, Better call an' wake Bone an' his brother, the ranger."

"Oh, damn, Roger that, 22. Need a 129?"

"That's affirmative."

"Unit 22 this is unit 27. We are en route. ETA five minutes, Code 3."

"Roger that, 27."

Newman turned to Sandra. "Get the tape, secure the area, Wanda an' Juan are on the way. Lauri is contacting Bone and Ranger Bone…probably Loraine, too." He looked down at the body in the grass. "Looks like we got another one."

"Should we go down an' check the body?"

"Not unless you want to piss off Bone…it wouldn't be pretty. He doesn't like anyone, an' I mean anyone, trackin' up his crime scene."

BONE RANCH

"What?...What?...What? Who? Oh, Lauridarlin', what up?...Oh, no, no, I'm awake...am now, anyway."

Tyrin, the blond and white pit bull he inherited from Lucy, along with the ranch when she was rescued by her people from her planet earlier this year, raised his head from beside Bone's leg, looked at him, yawned, laid his head back down and promptly went back to sleep.

"What? A 187? At Leonard Park?...Same MO?...Oh, damn. Call my brother...Uh, never mind he's here at the ranch with me and Padrino. We'll be there in twenty minutes...Call Loraine, she can get there before us...Tell Newman to seal the area...Ah, already has, good boy...Laterbye."

He jumped out of bed causing Tyrin to raise his head briefly once more, and then the ninety pound dog flopped over on his back, legs in the air.

"T-Bone! Rise and shine! Get your ass in gear...Got another one."

From across the hall came the muffled sound from his brother. "Ah, damn...I'm up, I'm up."

Bone quickly pulled on his black BDUs snapped his belt around his waist with his 500 and leather case of three speed loads. He slipped a white T-shirt over his head, stepped in a pair of loafers, without socks, grabbed his jacket and rubbed Tyrin's belly.

"I'm gone, brother." He shouted from down the hall.

"Right behind you."

Padrino wearing a pair of white skivvies, poked his head out of his bedroom.

"Got another one?

"Yep, looks like the same guy. Be back when I get back."

"Need to shut this guy down."

"That's the plan, Padrino, that's the plan."

He grabbed the keys to his Thing and headed out the back door on a dead run.

Bone jumped in, started the engine, grabbed his portable magnetic red bubble light, put it on the dash and spun out of the yard in first gear for the twenty mile trip into town.

"Come on, girl, let's make it in fifteen."

His tail lights disappeared down the caliche ranch road toward highway 51.

T-Bone was out the front door and in his state issued plain black wrapper sedan before Bone made it to the highway.

LEONARD PARK

Bone was waved through the entrance by Sergeant Hung twelve minutes after he left his ranch. He pulled down the lane and around to the west side of the zoo and parked behind the four flashing light units from the department and an EMT wagon.

Loraine walked up to him. "Took you long enough. I've been here for ten minutes already."

"See you didn't take time to put on your makeup."

"Kiss my ass, Bone."

"Looked at the scene yet?"

"Waitin' on you...Grandma's slow, but she's old."

"Bite me."

"In your dreams."

They walked up to Corporal Newman.

"Talk to me," said Bone.

"Haven't touched a thing. Didn't even go down to check the vic...It was obvious she was dead."

"Bless you."

"Parker an' I were on patrol through the park and heard the animals raisin' Billy-hell. Came over, looked around an' Parker spotted the body down the embankment, almost to the creek."

T-Bone walked up behind them. "Shall we go down an' take a look at the vic, brother?"

Bone nodded. "Why we're here."

They walked a good ten yards along the road before they worked their way down the levee so they wouldn't disturb any possible signs the perpetrator might have left directly above the body.

When they got down to the edge of the creek, they headed toward the body.

Bone knelt down beside her. "Same, same, except this is a white girl with henna hair."

There was a slight blood stain showing underneath the body.

Bone lifted one of her arms. "No rigor yet...Fresh." He looked up at Tiny. "She's been dead less than two hours...sizable lump on the back of her head."

The two men rolled the body to the side. Tiny held his light directly on the victim in addition to the lights from above.

"Yep, bruising around the neck, laryngeal prominence crushed...breasts excised, still oozing some...lot of grass and dead leaves stuck to the congealed blood and adipose tissue...Our boy's been busy." He looked up the slope. "See any sign where he carried her down?"

Tiny panned his tac light side to side all the way to the top. "Nothin'...No bent grass, footprints...Nothin'."

Bone looked at his younger brother. "He brought her by boat and dumped her on the bank...He's playing with us."

§§§

CHAPTER EIGHT

GAINESVILLE

Newman turned south on Weaver Street as the sun began to turn the eastern sky pink and send red and gold arrows shooting from the horizon.

His rookie partner, Sandra Parker, glanced over at him. "Again? I thought we checked the soccer fields at 0200."

"We did. Something's been bugging me for the last hour since we left the Zoo."

"What's that?"

"Been cogitating on how the murderer could get to the Zoo by boat."

"And?"

"Elm Fork of the Trinity is not that high unless it rains, so he'd have a real shallow draft boat, maybe like a jon boat. He could either go up stream or down...Up stream leads to Lindsay...Out of our jurisdiction, by the way."

"Okay, Sherlock. Where could he put in and get downstream?"

Parker didn't know the area very well.

"That's just it. There's an old low water crossing just past the Conseco Park and the water treatment plant." He pointed in the direction they were traveling. "A flood took some of it out a few years back, and the county decided not to replace it...You can't drive across it, and it blocks boat traffic when the water is low."

"How far is it from the crossing to where the body was found?" Parker looked to her right as they passed the water treatment plant. She could see the lights of a pair of eighteen wheelers driving north on I-35 in the background.

"Maybe three quarters of a mile...at the outside."

"Possible."

"That's what my gut tells me...Bone always says go with your gut."

They passed the last turnoff into the municipal soccer fields. The cruiser headlights illuminated a barbed wire fence and metal bow gate ahead—it was standing open.

"Oh crap." Newman's eyes narrowed.

"It wasn't like that four hours ago."

"No kiddin'. Another three or four hundred yards to the crossing as I recall...Check your side for a lock that's been cut off but don't get out of the car."

"Evidence?"

"You're learnin'...footprints, and fingerprints. Possible crime scene connected with that homicide."

"Right." Sandra rolled down her window and pulled out a powerful LED flashlight plus turned on the big mounted spot.

Newman stopped at the gate and looked for foot prints on his side where the gate hinge was but found none. "Figures…You got anything on your side?"

"I see a lock cut by bolt cutters…Couple foot prints."

"We'll have investigators cast 'em if they're decent."

He put the unit in drive and drove slowly to the Elm Creek crossing. He turned on the high beams.

Trees covered the roadway from both sides, making a rather spooky tunnel as they arched and grew into a solid canopy overhead. The shallow water of the creek glistened from the lights reflecting from it.

Sandra panned the spotlight attached in front of her door.

A small Navy surplus yellow inflatable boat was lit up by the lights. It had an electric trolling motor on the back, and more importantly, a crimson smear of dried blood on the near gunwale.

Newman let out a sigh. "Dammit, sometimes I hate it when I'm right."

GAINESVILLE POLICE DEPARTMENT
CRIME INVESTIGATOR'S UNIT

Loraine got to the office first, as the Bone brothers had to drive all the way to the ranch to shave, change into their regular day clothes, and come back. She had returned to her apartment only a few blocks from the station to shower and apply a modicum of makeup.

It was slightly after 0600, and she went to the break room to brew a fresh pot of coffee. The short night's sleep was taking its toll.

Back in the Inspector's Unit, Loraine flipped open her laptop, and suddenly had a thought.

"Dang it. Forgot to record yesterday's episode of my food blogger and podcaster." She opened up a Firefox browser and typed in *America's Favorite.*

The autofill added the word *Chef.* She hit *enter* and the software opened the link automatically. Loraine logged into the subscription site and began to search for the previous day's program.

"Bingo…Chicken Cacciatore…love that. Let's see how she makes it."

She hit play button on the screen with her mouse and the former runway model appeared and began her introduction, "Hi, everybody...I'm Chrystal Towers and today, on *America's Favorite Chef,* I'll be making one of my all time crowd pleasers...Chicken Cacciatore..."

Cascading locks of thick blond hair framed her picture perfect face. Her bright blue eyes and perfect smile reminded many people of a young Farrah Fawcett—except for the fact that she was almost six feet tall, had significantly larger breasts and a stunning hourglass figure. And she could cook, really, really well.

Loraine watched for tips on cutting technique as Chrystal set one red and one yellow bell pepper on her thick cutting board made from laminated bamboo. The whole process of slicing, coring, and dicing the two vegetables took less than twelve seconds.

"Gosh, she makes it look so friggin' easy." Loraine checked her watch. "Coffee's ready. Need an infusion of caffeine after last night," she mumbled.

She hit *pause* and pushed back to get her morning fix.

In less than a minute, she was back and savoring the aroma of Bone's special blend.

"Mmm…beats the heck out of the bargain brands that the department supplies," she murmured, took a satisfying sip and closed her eyes to savor the moment.

"So nice." Loraine put the mug down and resumed the video blog.

The Bone brothers darkened the office doorway as Loraine was on her second cup. Bone grinned when he smelled a familiar aroma.

"Hey, Shortcakes, like that new coffee?"

"Yeah, of course…sure you don't mind? It's kinda expensive."

"*Mi casa , su casa*, and all that rot. I got money. The boys at Black Rifle Coffee company earned my business…Life's too short to drink insipid joe."

"Got an extra mug, little big brother?" T-Bone grinned.

"Sure, if you don't mind a Marine Corps emblem on it."

The ranger laughed. "Special Forces guys don't mind slumming from time to time…Keeps us humble…or so they say."

Bone dug into his bottom drawer for a spare, dumped a handful of change out of in, and then handed it to Tiny along with his regular mug. "While you're up."

"Still black?"

"Is a bullfrog waterproof?"

"Two mugs of mud, on the way." T-Bone left for the break room.

"Whatcha watchin', Double D?" Bone craned his neck to see her screen.

"*America's Favorite Chef*...a great blog, podcast...and wonderful recipes."

"How come I never heard of it?"

"Cause you don't watch cooking shows...Don't need to, I guess...Plus you don't watch TV, except for the occasional football games."

"Point...What's he making?"

"Not a he...Definitely not a he." Loraine grinned.

"At the slightest risk of soundin' chauvinistic...perish the thought...All great chefs are, by and large...males."

"Okay, cave man. Check this out." Loraine turned the laptop slightly to the left so that her partner could see and hit *enter*.

The camera panned from a sauté pan with bell peppers and onions sizzling in olive oil to the bamboo cutting board. A pair of graceful woman's hands turned a peeled carrot lengthwise, split it, split the halves, and turning the four sections crossways, proceeded to dice it with the chef's knife.

She used the blade to add the root vegetables to the pan. When she was done, she laid the knife on the board.

"Wow, did you see that?" Bone was clearly impressed.

"Something about her technique? Trust me, that's not speeded up. That's her real time Executive Chef speed."

"Not that...look at the knife! You know who made that?"

Loraine hit the pause button. "How the heck could anybody know who made that knife?"

"His name is *Takeshi Saji*...one of the Master Craftsmen in Japanese cutlery...Lay odds the handle design is called Wind and Thunder Gods by Master *Kouichiro Tsukada*."

Loraine sat there slack-jawed. "How do you come up with that crap? You did it on that cask-aged Scotch that Jimmy Jack drank, too."

"So sue me. Can't help it if my brain remembers stuff better than other people's do." Bone shrugged.

T-Bone returned with the two coffees in one massive hand and a stack of donuts on a paper plate. "New delivery, fresh from the little shop on North Grand, the dispatcher said."

Loraine shook her head. "I really shouldn't."

Bone nodded. "Me neither...I'll take two chocolate glazed, bro."

Tiny grinned. "Okay, three for me, if ya'll insist."

Loraine pouted for a split second. "Oh, hell. Gimme honey glazed...This cooking show has got me kinda hungry."

Tiny passed her one on a blue paper napkin.

"They're kinda good...Ate two already. What are you watchin'?"

"Some chick cutting veggies with a $2,000 knife." Bone chuckled.

"Two thousand dollars? For one knife? Are you crazy?" Loraine was floored.

"Actually, a little over $2,300, with shipping. Saw it on-line." Bone took a bite out of his first donut and then washed it down with his favorite coffee.

Bone was nearly finished with his second donut. "Hey let's see what Miss Ginzu Knives looks like. Bet she's an oriental with a round face and short black hair."

"Think so, do you?" Loraine grinned. "You just want to make fun of my cooking blog."

"No seriously, she's got some high dollar gear, and the girl knows how to slice and dice...Curious as to what she looks like."

"Wanna bet a six pack of Michelob Ultra on it?" Loraine sat back in her chair.

"You wouldn't bet if you thought you could lose."

T-Bone shook his head. "Don't be such a stinkin' tightwad, Darrell. It's only a six pack. You thinks she's Oriental...put your money where your pie hole takes you."

Loraine giggled and gave Tiny a high five. "I like this guy. You need to bring him around more often...Darrell."

He shot her a look. Nobody called him *Darrell*.

"Okay, Sugar Britches, you're on...Six pack."

She tapped the enter key on her keypad. Loraine crossed her arms and was grinnin' like a Cheshire cat in a Friskies' commercial.

A few seconds later, the pleasant, but disembodied, voice turned into a half body frontal view of a smiling Chrystal Towers talking about the next step in the recipe.

The sight of the waspwaisted, buxom blond with golden tresses, caused Bone's jaw to drop.

"Close your mouth, Pard, before a fly drops in there...By the way, I like my Michelob Ultra cold...Real cold."

T-bone shook his head. "Would you look at that! She's seriously fine in places where most gals don't have places."

Bone chuckled. 'Got me on that one, Pard. Guess I need to do me a little Googlin' on that woman...Where's her show out of?"

"Would you believe Ardmore, Oklahoma...just thirty-five miles north?"

"What's her name?…And you say she can cook?"

"Chrystal Towers…and I'd say so."

"Chrystal Towers? Bet a donut it's a stage name…"

Bone's cell rang. He picked it up and looked at the caller ID. "Hey, Lauridarlin'. Top of the mornin' to you."

The smile on his face faded as she reported Newman's find at the creek.

A few seconds later, he responded, "We're on it…Laterbye." He turned to his cohorts. "Saddle up, muchachos."

An hour later, Bone wiped the soles of his Lucchese boots on the lawn beside the sidewalk leading to the back door of the station.

"Dang it. Dead leaves and organic matter   stick tighter'n a tick sometimes."

He swiped his electronic security badge on the lock and held the door open for Loraine and his brother. "*Entrez, s'il-vous-plaît.*"

"T-Bone's manners must be rubbing off on you." Loraine eyes telegraphed a bit of mischievousness.

"Whatever. Get in there, bubble butt, 'for I change my mind."

Tiny laughed. "Can I be the best man? Ya'll gotta remember to let me know way ahead of time."

"Cut the crap, T-Bone. We don't even like each other."

"Yeah, yeah. Keep tellin' yourself that, brother...Tuxedo or Western Casual?" Tiny tossed a playful left jab to Bone's midsection.

Loraine looked back over her left shoulder. The smile on her face faded as uncertainty crept in. *What's he seeing that we don't.*

Back in the Inspector's Unit office, Bone used a USB cable and downloaded the dozens of crime scene photos from the latest murder victim and the boat from his Galaxy 7.

Before he was done, the phone rang. He checked the caller ID. *Doc Fisk* Bone tapped the green icon and opened the speaker phone option.

"Greeting and salutations to the Prince of Pathology...You're up early."

"A hound dog howdy to the Duke of Detectives. Chief Anderson called me at home around six thirty."

T-Bone looked at Loraine and mouthed the words, "Duke of Detectives?"

She chuckled and waved her hand, signaling, "Tell you later."

Bone groaned silently. "Seems the heat is on the old man. One thing to have a killing out in the county...Inside the city limits, particularly with a serial killer, things get hotter by the minute...My gut tells me the mayor called him first."

"Whatever...I don't have the hospital call me when a DB is delivered to the morgue in the middle of the night." Fisk laughed. "Like I told the Captain, they'll still be dead when I get there."

Bone chuckled. "You're so sensitive, just like me, Doc...By the way, anything show up in tox screens yet?"

"I was getting to that. The first two were negative for illegal drugs. Gals were clean as a whistle. Still waiting on number three...Just finished the crack and peel on number four.

Fracture of the lamboid suture, seam on the posterior of the skull...Perp whacked her pretty hard."

"Laceration associated with the head trauma?"

"Negatory on that, good buddy. Contact was consistent with a non-rigid tool."

"Like a leather covered sap, perhaps." Bone's eyes narrowed.

"Very likely. Not COD, though...Killer choked her down like the others."

"Bastard...Gotta nail him."

"Yeppers. Oh, almost forgot...Peach came by and took scrapings off the vic's feet, toes and nails...Send you the mp3 of the actual blow by blow, and high res photos for your case file."

"You da man, Doc...Oh, say, by the way. Just out of curiosity, are there any new doctors at the hospital?"

"Interesting you should ask, got a new one a little over a month ago...from Denver. A Doctor Stanley Albert Landrum, by name."

"What's his specialty?"

"Cosmetic surgery...specializing in breast augmentation...Why?"

"Like I said, just curious…Laterbye." Bone closed his eyes, sighed, and began drumming slowly on his forehead with his trigger finger.

Loraine glanced at Tiny and whispered, "Cogitating."

T-Bone nodded and smiled. "Been doin' that since we were kids."

§§§

CHAPTER NINE

GOVERNOR'S LOUNGE

The lounge was decorated for Halloween. Jack-o'-lanterns were placed at intervals along the thirty-five foot bar, and orange and black streamers were draped across the antique tin ceiling. Fake spiderwebs were strung across the front windows. There were candles stuck in longnecks on all the tables. A plastic, full-size skeleton was seated in a chair at one of the tables with an unlit cigarette in between his teeth, and his bony fingers wrapped around a Lone Star longneck.

Chucky dolls and clown heads hung from the ceiling while Vertis was dressed in a complete witches' costume, including a pointed hat. A witches' broom leaned against the back bar.

A sign over the bar read: *Halloween Mask Night. All patrons must wear a mask, no costume, just a mask to enter the Governor's Lounge.*

There were all types of masks around the club, even some of only heavy makeup.

Loraine wore a Morticia Adams mask, Stella, a Lizzie Borden, Wanda's was an alien gray, and Juan Gomez, Freddie Kruger. St. John had a replica of Michael Myer's mask from *Halloween*—that very few people knew was actually a death mask of Willian Shatner as Captain Kirk—and Peach's was Vampira.

Vertis was playing *Monster Mash* on the jukebox.

Bone and Tiny came through the door, both wore half-masks of the lower part of an elephant, including the trunk.

"Hey, Bone, T-Bone, thought ya'll were goin' to wear masks," said Loraine.

"Har, har, good thing you didn't wear Morticia's dress, you'd never be able to walk."

"Up your's, Bone...I'm ready for my Michelob Ultra."

"Touche, Pard...Vertis, set Morticia here up with up to a six pack of Michelob Ultra."

"Lost another bet, did you?"

"Could say."

"What are you an' T-Bone havin'?...I'm assumin' that's who that is behind that mask." Vertis giggled.

"You could tell?" asked Tiny.

"Just a wild guess."

"Couple of Shiner's," said Bone.

"How're you gonna drink 'em with those trunks hangin' down?" asked Stella.

"Oh, right...bring straws."

"Oh, my God." Vertis shook her head, and reached into the cooler under the bar for the Shiners.

Monster Mash finished on the jukebox and Ginny Mac, dressed as a Gothic vampire slayer, tuned the audience up with *Highway to Hell*.

Bone got up from the table and lumbered for the back. "Head call."

St. John waited until he disappeared down the hall. He pulled a bottle of Louisiana Hot Sauce from his pocket, grabbed Bone's beer which was a little over half full, dumped most of the small bottle of liquid fire into the top. The captain wiped the mouth of Bone's beer and put the hot sauce back in his pocket.

Bone sauntered from the back and took his seat at the table. "Ah, the pause that refreshes...Miss me?"

"You wouldn't believe," replied Loraine.

He grabbed his beer, turned it up, guzzled it down, set the empty back on the table and belched. "Mmm, good." Bone chuckled. "Reminds me of a girl I dated once, named Mary Marie Goode...called her M-m Good...fit too."

Loraine backhanded him across the chest. "Bone, that's so crude."

"Somethin' we've all come to expect an' love," said Stella. "How was your beer?"

"Must have been one of those new flavors Shiner's testing. Had a nice kick to it...Need another." He held up his finger to Vertis and circled the air.

Ginny Mac started a sultry version of *Put a Spell on You* as Vertis stepped over to the table.

"Round for the table, Bone?"

"Set 'em up, Vertis, on my tab."

"Your tab looks like the national debt now, Bone."

"It's okay, I'll just raise taxes."

"What are you, a liberal Democrat?"

Bone slaps his chest with his fist like he'd been shot. "Oh, oh, got me, good shot Vertis."

She turned to go to the bar to get a tray of beer. "I wish."

"None for me, Vertis...Got the early shift in the mornin'...had enough," said Stella as she got to her feet. "No rest for the weary."

"I think that's wicked, Stella," said Jose Sanchez.

She flipped him off as she headed to the door. "See you in the mornin' Julio, an' don't be late."

The same white Ford van that was parked across the street in the shadows a couple of days earlier was there again. A large man sat inside as before, watching Stella's small rent house.

Her light blue Honda CRV pulled up into the drive and Stella got out. She had removed her Lizzie Borden mask and had it in her hand as she walked back to the hatch and raised it to get her go bag to take in the house, *Need to clean my sidearm before I go to bed.*

The man slipped up behind her as she leaned in to get her bag. He struck the back of her head with his leather sap.

Stella slumped forward, half into the open rear of her car. The big man picked her up, carried her to the van parked in the shadows. He opened the back, grabbed a roll of duct tape, rolled her inside and taped her mouth, hands, and feet.

GAINESVILLE PD

Officer Sanchez stood beside Dispatcher Lauri's station.

"Try Stella again, Lauri, she's over thirty minutes late... Stella is never late. If she was sick, she would have called me...She was fine when she left the club last night...I called her house an' her cell, no answer."

"Okay, but, this is the third time. She's apparently not near her radio." Lauri spoke into her mike. "Bravo 1-77, this is Dispatch, please respond...Stella? Please respond."

There was only open air sound coming from the speaker.

"All right, Lauri...thanks."

She frowned. "Sorry."

Sanchez walked down the hall to Captain St. John's office and knocked on the door jam.

"Enter."

Jose entered and stood in front of the captain's desk.

St. John looked up at the officer. "What is it, Sanchez?"

"Uh...Captain, I'm kinda concerned about Stella. She's never been late before, and we can't raise her on her radio...Told me last night when she left the club for me not to be late this morning for our shift."

"You call her home?"

"Yessir, no response."

St. John keyed his intercom. "Lauri, send a unit by Officer Johnson's home and check it out."

"Just did that, sir. Her vehicle is there, hatch open, her go bag with her weapon was in it, and the mask she wore last night was laying on the ground...but no response at the door."

"Have the unit enter...on my responsibility."

"Yessir."

St. John looked up at Sanchez. "Maybe she just overslept."

"No sir, not in this lifetime...Stella is more Gung ho than anyone on the force."

The captain spun his chair around, looked out the window and muttered, "Yeah, I know."

Lauri's voice came over the intercom, "Captain, her house was empty...bed not slept in."

"Lauri, notify all units that we have an officer unaccounted for...Make that an APB...Bone! Get in here!"

Bone walked down the hall and entered St. John's office.

"What's up, Boss?"

"Stella's missing and unaccounted for. I've issued an APB…"

"Crap…She's a blonde…I'm on it."

He spun on his heel and headed back down to the Inspector's Unit.

St. John looked at the concerned young officer still in front of his desk. "Hit the streets, Sanchez. Maybe it's nothin', but we can't chance it…Now, get out of my sight!"

"Yessir."

The captain turned in his chair and stared out the window again, this time with a very worried expression.

§§§

CHAPTER TEN

RADIO HUT

Officer Sanchez walked through the front door and approached the large clerk. He glanced at the plastic name tag on his light blue long sleeve Radio Hut shirt—BERNIE LIPSCHITZ.

"Mister Lipschitz, sorry to bother you, but an Officer Johnson was in here a few days ago—good lookin' blonde...friendly."

"Yessir, I recall."

"So, did you notice anything suspicious?"

The big man got a puzzled expression. "Like what?"

"Well, like maybe someone following her when she left or watchin' her from outside...or anything, anything at all?"

He thought for a moment and shook his head. "No, sorry, officer...Golly, is something wrong?"

"I'm not at liberty to say, sir...Thank you for your time." Sanchez glanced down at his name tag again and smiled. "Bet you got a lot of teasin', growin' up."

Bernie returned the smile. "You wouldn't believe." He pursed his lips. "Every day of my life."

Sanchez grabbed hold of the door handle, and then looked back. "I'll bet...Well, thank you for your time."

"Yes, sir, anytime."

GAINESVILLE POLICE DEPARTMENT
FORENSICS LAB

Peach Presley noted the various bits of grain she could identify under the microscope's display on her monitor—identical to the others. She blinked twice and turned to enter the results in her official electronic report.

She took another sip of strong black coffee. "Wakey, wakey. Gosh, wish I had slept better last night."

Dragging her cell phone from her lab frock pocket, she scrolled through her contacts and stopped in the Bs. She hit the big man's speed dial.

He answered immediately. "Bone. Make it quick."

"No need to be so short with me. I didn't put the hot sauce in your Shiner...Wanted to give...."

"Not now...Stella's missing."

"What do you mean missing? When? How?"

"Briefing room...Now. Don't be late."

The connection dropped before she could say a word. Her mind raced. Suddenly, the thought of her best friend lying on the table at Doc Fisk's became a real possibility. Her heart pounded. She clenched her teeth.

Slowly, Peach unbuttoned the white lab smock. She stepped to the corner of the lab and hung the coat on a hook, exposing the Cruel Girl jeans and chambray shirt underneath. She opened her locker and took out a black ballistic nylon gun belt with a Glock 19 in a carbon fiber holster. Peach pulled the slide back and let it fly into battery with a 9mm round.

She buckled the gun belt on and adjusted the holster on her hip. In twenty seconds, the Georgia Peach became a Steel Magnolia. She grabbed her pocketbook and turned off the lights as she left.

ST. JOHN'S OFFICE

The captain keyed his intercom. "Lauri, get me Stanton on the phone."

"Right away, sir."

St. John drummed his fingers on his desk top. "Wanda's on one, sir."

"Thanks, Lauri...He picked up his desk phone and punched the flashing button. "Wanda, hate to wake you, know you had a long night…but, Stella's missing…"

WANDA'S HOUSE

Wanda sat bolt upright in bed, her cell phone in one hand, and she was rubbing her eyes and her face with the other.

She blinked several times, still trying to wake up. "What?…What'd you mean, missing, Captain?…She was at…"

"Just what I said…she didn't show up for her shift this morning. I'm calling in all available personnel…Know you had the late shift, that's why you're the last on the list to call."

Wanda looked down at the screen on her phone to check the time. "Oh, God…She never misses her shift…Give me five an' I'm rolling."

"Knew I could count on you…There's a briefing in five here at the station…You can make it, if you hustle."

"Got it…I'll be there."

She punched the off button on the side of her phone, jumped up and sprinted to her bathroom."

RECIPE FOR MURDER

GAINESVILLE PD

The briefing room was standing room only.
Captain St. John, both Bone brothers, and Loraine
stood at the front. An official color photograph of
Stella in uniform was projected on the front video
monitor.

Wanda entered the room and took a seat at the
back.

St. John nodded at her and opened the briefing.
"Guys, we have good reason to believe Corporal
Stella Johnson was abducted late last night after
she left the Governor's Lounge. We just put out an
APB. I'm turning over the immediate search to
Detective Bone.

"Until Chief Anderson returns from temporary
medical leave, which should last a few more
days..."

A tittering of chuckles ran through the room.

"...I will be running this department and
coordinating efforts with Cooke, Grayson, and
Denton counties and their associated PDs...You all
know how urgent this is...Don't let me down."

St. John's eyes misted over as he pursed his lips. "Don't let Stella down...Let's bring her home." He turned to Bone, nodded once, and left the room.

Bone approached the podium. He towered over it as he said, "People, I ain't gonna sugar coat this. We have an active serial killer in the area, and it's highly probable that he has our Stella."

He paused for a second as several gasps came from the assembled cops. "Here are a few pics from the four known crime scenes...Not pretty...just fair warning."

He picked up the remote control for the projector hooked up to his laptop. "Victim number one, Denton county." Bone showed a nude woman as found, then clicked on the one of her on her back with the breasts gone.

"Oh my God." One of the female officers brought her hand to her mouth and closed her eyes tightly.

"Grayson county...three days later." Bone showed them as well, before he proceeded to the one in rural Cooke County.

He continued quickly, "Also this week...right here in the city limits...Here's number four."

One of the female officers began sobbing softly. Her partner put his arm around her.

"What we know is that the breasts were removed with a scalpel or something similar…and with some degree of skill. Also, the first three vics all had crushed grain dust of livestock feed residue on their feet. As you might find in a feed store, grain mill, or possibly even a barn."

"Crap. That's a lot of places in this part of Texas." Rick Gore shook his head.

Peach held up her hand.

Bone nodded. "Peach."

"I finished the analysis of the scrapings on vic four just before this meeting was called…"

"And?"

"All the traces were identical…I mean absolutely identical."

Bone pursed his lips. "That means at least three and four were kept, and most likely killed, in the same place…That helps, Thanks, Peach…The killer strangled each victim…Logically, we conclude he has very strong hands. Vics were not sexually assaulted and there were no fingerprints or DNA…Now you know what we know."

Bone's cell rang—he frowned. "Bone...Doc Fisk...Got anything?" He put his phone on speaker.

"Confirmation on the surgical removal of the breasts, Bone, like the others...Definitely a thin bladed scalpel, or razor...and somebody knew their stuff."

"Gracias, Doc...Oh, let's keep the autopsy findings QT."

"This ain't my first week, Bone."

"Yeah." He punched his cell off and looked back up.

"Any psychological profile yet?" Juan Gomez asked.

"Good question. I'll turn it over to my ranger brother." Bone motioned to T-Bone to move to the podium.

"I'm Texas Ranger Tiny Bone. Our department psychologist is working on that angle. He's asked for assistance from the FBI...Neither has come up with a full blown profile...as of yet."

Bone stepped back in. "We don't have the luxury of time for a psychological hunt. *If* Stella is still alive, we have to find her before the butcher acts out his little psychopathic drama."

The word *if* sent shivers through several officers. A single tear rolled down Peach's left cheek and darkened her chambray blouse as her jaw muscles rippled.

Bone clicked on the remote. Two images appeared. On the left was a map of Gainesville. "Here's the search grid pattern Tiny and I came up with. On the right is a roster with assignments to the various blocks. Printouts of these are available from the dispatcher on your way out."

Loraine stepped up. "One other thing…if there is an asterisk in your search block, that means there's a business, store, or restaurant that Stella may have visited in the last two weeks. Get that breakdown from dispatch as well."

"Thanks, Pard. Briefing dismissed. Let's get movin' people."

The room cleared except for Moomer, Rick, Tiny, Loraine, and Bone.

"What's the plan, Mone? You didn't put Gore and me on the search roster?"

"That's because I want you guys to go over the Feed mill in Muenster with a fine tooth comb.

Every room, every one of those round metal storage silos."

"Muenster is out…"

Bone cut Rick off. "I know where it is…Screw the jurisdiction. Know the owner…Good guy. We gotta check it anyway. Get a move on."

Loraine could see Bone's mind working overtime. "How 'bout us?"

"You're with me. Gonna hit the big mill in Valley View first. It'll take a while…it's huge. Then we'll split up, and you'll take the abandoned Starlight Feed Store on Old Denton Road…Know where that is?"

She nodded.

Bone turned to his brother. "T-Bone, I'll give you three, cause they're smaller and a lot closer together. Ward's on West Broadway…Tom's Feed and Seed on North Commerce, and the old Smith Brothers out on Burns City Road…Been closed for years."

"Got it. Ya'll be careful, hear?" Tiny's jaw was set, and his face was a study in determination.

He and Bone bumped fists. Tiny turned and walked quickly away.

Bone looked down at Loraine. "Am I forgetting anything, Double D?"

"Not that I see. Great plan on short notice…If I think of anything, I'll holler."

"Lets' roll." The pair quickly left the nearly deserted building…

§§§

CHAPTER ELEVEN

TOM's FEED AND SEED

Ranger Bone wheeled into the narrow parking area beside the main building at the largest feed, fertilizer, and seed supplier in Gainesville. There was only twenty feet between the curb on North Commerce Street and the front of the building.

Tiny stepped out and donned his silverbelly Stetson as he closed the door on his unmarked car.

It didn't take long to figure out where the main office was, even though the veteran lawman had never entered the premises before. Down the broad hallway to his left were sacks of fertilizer—to the right was the grain auger and dump chute that filled either pickup trucks or tow-behind spreader trailers. Eighteen wheelers had a separate loading area and truck scale on the north side of the complex.

T-Bone ducked as he entered the 84 inch tall doorway leading to the office and sales area. He brought himself to his full height once inside, and his gaze dropped on a twenty-three year old engrossed in a *Western Horseman* magazine.

The sole salesman jumped with a start as he became aware of the huge man towering seven feet, with boots and hat, over him. He dropped the magazine and stammered his routine greeting, "Can I...can...can I help you, sir?"

"Sure hope so. I'm Texas Ranger Bone assigned to investigate a felony crime here in Cooke County."

T-Bone purposely lowered the pitch in his natural voice to sound more intimidating. He needn't have bothered. His bulk, height and the custom 1911 on his right hip did the job quite nicely.

He held out his cell phone with a color picture of Stella in civilian clothes. "Have you seen this woman in the past few days?"

The hapless clerk was already shaking before he saw the pic. "No, no sir. Not me."

Tiny pocketed the phone. "Mind if I look around? It's a matter of life and death."

"Sure. What do you need to see?"

T-Bone walked over the office door and held it open. "Everything."

"Sure, ask me whatever," the man blurted. "Anything you need."

COOKE COUNTY

Bone glanced over at Loraine, who sat in the right seat with her arms crossed. They were still several miles from Valley View, and traffic was fairly heavy on Interstate 35 for that time of day.

"You and Stella were pretty close, right?"

"We *are* still pretty close. Don't talk like she's dead, at least not yet."

"So sorry...Really, I am. What I mean is you've been teaching her martial arts for a couple of years, right? Ya'll spend a lot of time together outside of work."

"Sure. She's working on her brown belt. She wants to be a black before next summer's competition."

"So she's good."

"Oh, you bet she is...Did you know she was a competitive gymnast for over twelve years?" Loraine smiled. "Girl's a natural athlete. Fierce competitor. She ranked second in all of Texas her senior year."

"Uh-huh, knew that."

Bone smiled at the memory of the diminutive blonde bombshell blasting away with his monster revolver, "Theodore"—AKA "Teddy." for short.

He signaled for the second exit to Valley View, a small town of less than 1,000 people on poker flat farming country sited at the edge of a winding valley on two sides. He lifted off the throttle and the somewhat boxy VW Thing slowed quickly from 80 MPH.

Bone kept the open top roadster around 55 on the short section of access road to the aptly named Easy Street overpass. He made a power-on left hand drift onto the deserted bridge and repeated the maneuver again to the northbound access.

Loraine was holding on to her armrests with white knuckles. "Ever think about a career with NASCAR?"

He shook his head. "Told me I was too tall...their loss." He ran through the gears, downshifted twice, braked hard for the parking lot entrance, and slid to a stop in the gravel lot by the office. "We're here."

His partner breathed sigh of relief. "Thank, God...Next time we take my Mustang."

Bone grabbed his hat and stepped out before she unbuckled her seat belt. "You coming or what?"

Inside the mill head office, Bone introduced himself to the secretary-receptionist. She led him to the office of the Chief Operating Officer, Martin Otto.

The big man gave a cursory explanation of why they needed to check the entire facility. The words *life and death* seemed to make the difference.

Martin quickly acceded to their rather strange demand, but got up, and grabbed a white hard hat off a peg sticking out of a walnut plaque in his office.

The three went back out to the reception area. Martin opened a cabinet and retrieved a pair of similar hard hats and three packages of foam ear plugs. "Everybody has to wear these inside the plant...OSHA rules."

Bone didn't bother arguing as it might take too much time. He sat his cowboy hat upside down atop the cabinet and donned the short billed plastic one. It was way too small.

Loraine giggled.

The detective shot her a look and adjusted the sweat band inside the safety hat as far out as it would go. It was still a couple sizes too small. "One size fits all, they said." He pointed to the door. "Lead on, Mister Otto."

As they approached the inner workings of the mill itself, Martin passed out the ear plugs. Grinders and motors get kinda noisy. You'll want these, too. I'll show you every room, but it will take a while."

Loraine nodded.

Bone shot him a *thumbs up* sign.

They passed a room with a workman filling large burlap bags with premixed cattle feed, Bone tapped Loraine on the arm.

She looked at him quizzically.

He pointed to the floor. Around the electronic scale for weighing the bags as they were filled was a brown haze of crushed grain, salt, and dried molasses. Bone said nothing but rubbed his thumb against his middle and index finger.

She made the connection and frowned.

An hour later, they finished the walk-through of the mill—nothing.

All right, Pard, guess we can move on down the list. You go ahead and check out Starlight...I'll go to the old abandoned Johnson Mill on Broadway. You can join me soon as you can...I'll wait on you."

"Damn you, Bone, why do you get the closest?"

"It's the biggest, Pard...over six stories. Won't take ya'll long to check out the others, then join me. Take several of us to go through that thing."

Loraine puffed out her cheeks, blew her breath in exasperation and nodded. "Okay."

She looked up at the big man. "Getting really nervous, Bone, don't mind sayin'."

"Me too, Pard. But, we gotta check all these places...She could be almost anywhere."

"I know."

§§§

CHAPTER TWELVE

GAINESVILLE

"Kilo 12-36…Lauridarlin, you busy?"

"Never too busy for you, Bone."

"Contact Sheriff Brennan and have him send a unit to back up Loraine at that abandoned Starlight Feed store out on Old Denton Road…It's technically out of City anyway…She's checking it out first."

"Can do, Bone, got something?"

"Don't know yet, it's a shot. I'm headed to the old Johnson Mill…Ranger Bone is checking the old feed store out on Burns City Road."

"10-4, Bone…be careful."

"Always, Lauridarlin', always."

"Kilo 12-55. Do you copy?"

"Kilo 12-55. Go ahead Lauri."

The call from Dispatch interrupted Loraine in route to the Starlight Feed Store.

"We have a 27 at 3602 Garnett, homeowner requests an officer."

"That's Angel's house…I'm on it, Lauri, call Wanda for backup. Kilo 12-55 out."

Loraine pulled up to 3602 Garnett and saw the open garage door. A small girl, twelve years old, stood inside with her arms folded over her chest. Loraine got out of her unit and walked up the driveway into the garage.

A man laid on his stomach in the middle of the garage floor.

She turned to the slight-built blonde-headed child. "Hey, Angel, what's going on?"

The girl brought her hands together in front of her, left hand in a cup and right hand in a fist inside the cup. She bowed slightly, and then separated her hands, both into fists in front of her hips. "Master Loraine, I caught this...this person, trying to break into our house. He scared my little sister half to death...I had to deal with the situation." She straightened back up and re-crossed her arms.

"I see." Loraine looked down at the burglar. "Okay, bad ass, on your feet."

The burglar turned his face toward Loraine. Both eyes were black, there blood ran from his nose, his upper lip was swollen, and his left ear newly cauliflowered.

"I can't."

"What do you mean, 'you can't'?"

"She told me not to move."

A slight grin crept across Loraine's face. "She told you not to move?"

"Yeah, she said she would hurt me again if I moved...Don't want no more of that."

Officer Stanton pulled up, got out of her patrol unit, and walked into the garage.

Loraine bit her lower lip. "So, what do you think, Angel? Reckon you ought to let him up so Officer Stanton can take him to jail?...Your call."

Angel did not uncross her arms but looked down at the burglar. "Okay, you can get up now..." She squinted her eyes. "...but, I'd move real careful if I were you."

The man swallowed. "Yes, Ma'am."

He carefully got to his feet, limped over to Officer Stanton, turned around slowly, and stuck his hands behind him.

A grinning Stanton cuffed him.

"Ow, ow, ow...think she dislocated my shoulder."

Loraine tried to bite back another smile. "You're lucky that's all she did, scumbag. She's a first degree black belt, Kung Fu, and my star pupil."

Wanda shook her head. "Stupid goes all the way to the bone...Let's go sweet cheeks...You have the right to remain silent..."

She led the limping burglar down the drive to her unit.

Loraine turned to Angel. "Very good, grasshopper, you showed remarkable restraint...You learned well."

Angel bowed again, and repeated the hand movements. *"Doh je, Sifu*...I am honored you think so."

COOKE COUNTY

It was late afternoon by the time Tiny pulled up to the abandoned feed store on Burns City Road, south of Gainesville.

He got out, walked up to the front door, bent over, examined the ground, and then the lock. *Nothin'.*

It became obvious to him that no one had been here in a very long time—no tracks or undisturbed dust.

Tiny walked around to the back—same story.

"Water haul...Just as well, know where she's not," he muttered, turned and walked back around to the front to his vehicle, got in, checked the location off on his laptop, and left.

RECIPE FOR MURDER

STARLIGHT FEED STORE

Loraine pulled up to the old feed store, just north of Era on Highway 51.

Sheriff Deputy Harley Kerns, a thirty year old recent discharge from the Marines, still wearing the Corps regulation haircut, waited out front in his county unit.

Loraine got out of her vehicle. "Hey Harley...Thanks for meeting me."

"Hey, Loraine...what took you so long? Thought maybe you got lost."

"Not likely...Had to stop and handle a B and E...Some inbred picked the wrong house...My twelve year old star pupil almost beat him to death.

"Angel? Wow, you couldn't melt me and pour me on her."

Loraine grinned. "Yeah, she's definitely a walkin' deadly weapon."

"What's goin' on?"

"We think Stella may be being held in an abandoned feed mill or old feed store."

"Yeah, got the APB...Dang, like Stella, she's good people...Well, let's get started."

They walked toward the main building of the three that were part of the store.

An hour and a half later, Loraine and Harley headed toward their vehicles.

The deputy shook his head. "Well, that was a dry hole."

"Yeah, thanks anyway. It's another one off the list...Got to catch up with Bone and help go through the old Johnson Mill...all six stories."

"Ya'll need help, just holler...The sheriff said to give ya'll whatever you need."

"Gracias, Harley."

GAINESVILLE

Stella laid on a pile of old dusty gunny sacks at the bottom of a fourteen by fourteen foot elevator shaft, her mouth and feet were taped. Her hands were also taped behind her back.

The air was stale and musty but still permeated with the odor of cattle feed.

Stella, clad only in black thong panties and bra, opened her eyes, squinched them in pain from the knot on the back of her head. She tried to look around in the murky darkness. What light there was the rapidly fading sunlight from outside had dust motes dancing in it.

She could feel the coarse sacks against her back and legs. *Where are my clothes? ...Oh, God.*

Stella blinked a couple of times and turned her head. She could hear heavy footsteps come down some wooden stairs somewhere close by. Her eyes widened as the footsteps came closer...

GAINESVILLE

Wanda cruised her search area slowly. She saw a car pass going in the opposite direction with a blonde in the passenger seat.

"Dang, that looks like Stella." She popped her lights, did a U turn and gave chase.

The vehicle pulled over. Wanda got out, hurried to the driver's door and looked in. A blonde sat in the passenger seat, her hair was exactly like Stella's—but it wasn't her.

"Oh, I'm sorry, I thought you were someone else." She turned back to her squad car. "Have a nice day…Drive safely now."

JOHNSON MILL

Bone pulled up as the gloaming settled in and got out of his Thing. The top crest of a huge yellow full hunter's moon peeked above the eastern horizon.

He stepped over to a plain white Ford van also parked in front of the office section. Bone tried to look inside, but it was too dark. He pulled out his tac light and shined it through the glass, and then angled it to the back—nothing that he could see.

Bone put away the small light and walked to the gray metal door in the front, noticed it was not locked—he turned the knob and entered.

Bone turned on his powerful tac light again in the very dark and dusty office. He panned around the floor—tracks showed plainly in the dust past the counter. There were metal desks on the other side, and the tracks led beyond them through an open door in the back.

He moved to the side to avoid disturbing them and paused for a moment to study the prints. "Hmm…Big son of a gun…long gait, and he's carryin' something heavy," he muttered.

Bone shined his light around and through the door out into the big warehouse behind the office. The light picked up a glint from something just outside the door to the office.

The large area was currently being used as storage for collector antique cars lined up in rows. There were over thirty vintage automobiles in the building.

Bone recalled a gruesome story from back in the '50s when the manager of the mill had brought his nine year old son to the plant for the day. They had gotten on the large open-sided elevator that was used to move palleted feed from one floor to another in the six story building.

Unbeknownst to the father at the controls for the massive elevator, the curious boy, wearing a Brooklyn Dodgers T-shirt, looked over the side trying to peer down into the basement area that had big rubber cushions for underneath the elevator. The young lad's head was caught on the bottom of the second floor as the elevator rose, and was cleanly sheared from his body to fall back to the first floor.

The father was never the same after his son's death, and the mill closed less than a year later. It was said to be haunted.

Bone walked forward, bent over just outside the door, and picked up the item that had glinted in his light. It was Stella's small hideaway backup .22 pistol on a lanyard that she always wore around her neck lying on one of the many burlap sacks scattered about.

As he looked at the tiny weapon in his hand, a vision formed in his mind.

A large man in the shadows had an unconscious Stella over his shoulder like a sack of potatoes, and shuffled across the floor. Her hands, feet, and mouth were taped. She wore the same clothes as at the Halloween party. Stella's pistol necklace dropped from around her neck and landed on a burlap sack.

His godfather, Padrino, appeared to him in the vision. *"Look at nothing, my son, but see everything."*

§§§

CHAPTER THIRTEEN

JOHNSON MILL

Stella heard the heavy footsteps come closer and closer to her basement level chamber. Her heart beat like a jackhammer as adrenaline coursed through her veins. She tried to call out for help, but the silver duct tape was much too strong. Her breathing was rapid as she strained unsuccessfully against the multiple wraps of the same tape around her ankles.

In the dim light, she saw a huge dark shadow looming over her. She could barely make out his legs straddling her and a large hunting knife moving toward her breasts. Stella tried to push away from him with her legs, but her heels slipped on the loose pile of burlap bags.

The hulking man leaned over and laughed out loud as she squirmed harder and harder trying to wriggle her hands free.

The light was dim but a single, tiny beam reflected off the knife and onto his face. In a brief instant, she recognized the familiar face and her eyes grew open even wider. *You bastard!*

Her muffled scream seemed to delight her kidnapper.

"Hee, hee, hee...don't waste your breath, little girl. Nobody can hear you down here." He slipped the tip of the blade under her bra, right in between her well-formed breasts.

Suddenly, she kicked up as hard as she could with both feet right into the crotch of the man before he could snip her bra apart. There was a sickening squishing sound as Stella landed her double heel kick directly on his testicles.

GAINESVILLE

Tiny took the Burns City Road back into town, turned left at the stop sign, drove two blocks west, and then a right on Grand Avenue. He reached up and grabbed the radio mic from the dash.

"Ranger Bone to Kilo 12-36…Come in Bone."

He waited for a moment through the silence.

"Bone? Come in…Ranger Bone to Kilo 12-55. Loraine, you there? Come back."

"Kilo 12-55, go ahead Tiny."

"Just tried Bone on the radio…No response."

"Must be inside searching Johnson Mill…I'll try his cell."

"10-4, Tiny out."

JOHNSON MILL

The attacker screamed like a wounded hyena and dropped the knife. He toppled over to his left side, grabbed his crotch and moaned as intense pain racked his body.

Stella quickly tucked up, pulled her knees against her chest, and pushed her taped hands forward and underneath her feet. Straining as she hard as she could, the panicked cop pulled them up and over her feet.

GAINESVILLE

Loraine pulled over to the side of the road, stopped her car, took her phone from her purse, swiped the face, and then hit Bone's speed number. She could hear it ring as she held it up to her ear.

"Come on, come on."

JOHNSON MILL

Stella breathed so fast that she almost passed out from hyperventilation. She ripped the tape off her mouth, gasped for air—grabbed the blade, wedged the handle between her knees, and sliced the tape in two between her wrists.

Johnson glanced quickly at the man writhing in pain. She took the knife with her right hand and cut the tape between her legs, leaving a band of silver around each ankle as she sprang to her feet.

Stella didn't have a clue where she was. She couldn't see the stairs leading up to the ground floor and the others in the dark shadows. She brushed against a thick rope hanging down the middle of the elevator shaft.

The building's freight elevator had been removed years earlier following the death of the young boy. The rope was then used to lower salvageable items and equipment down to the bottom floor.

Corporal Johnson shot a quick glance at her kidnapper on his knees as he struggled to get to his feet.

"You evil little witch...I'll rip you limb from limb for what you did!" he wheezed.

Stella clenched the knife in her teeth, jumped as high as she could, grabbed the rope and began climbing hand-over-hand, her skills as a twelve year competitive gymnast came into play.

She saw moonlight streaming through the many windows up above her on the second floor and headed for it as fast as her arms would take her. She heard a guttural scream come from the dark hole below.

"You will never get away from me!"

Upstairs on the first floor, Bone had heard the man cry out. His eyes rapidly searched the huge open car storage area. He couldn't see the large opening where the freight elevator used to be because of all the cars as he panned his light around, and then sprinted in the direction of where he thought the sound came from. He heard the man's voice again.

The man staggered to his feet, still holding his crotch. He looked around and could barely make out the rope moving in the dim light.

He looked up and saw Stella's shadowy form almost to the third floor. The big man grabbed the old rope and started to shake it.

Stella wrapped her legs around the rope, twisting it around her right leg as the man shook the thick woven hemp violently back and forth trying to shake her loose.

160

Stella lowered her body to full extension, released the wrap, and started to swing her legs in time with his shaking.

After a couple of swings, she brought her legs together, piked them up into a horizontal position to her body and propelled herself toward the side when the swing reached its apex.

She released the rope, arched her body through the air, like in a paralled bar dismount, and landed on the third floor over eight feet from the opening of the shaft. Stella had no way of knowing Bone was three floors below her.

The man vented his rage when he saw her dim form disappear from the center of the shaft. He ran to the stairway and sprinted up.

Bone threaded his way through the cars until he reached the open elevator shaft on the first floor. He flashed his light at the movement of the rope in the center and aimed the beam down to the basement just below.

Bone could plainly see the cut pieces of tape. He glanced up, but couldn't see anyone on the rope, and then heard heavy footsteps on the stairs at the north side of the building and above him. He turned and sprinted through more cars to the stairwell at the north side of the big room.

Bone reached the door, jerked it open, and took two steps at a time up the old wooden stairway. His phone rang with his William Tell Overture ring tone. He reached down to his belt and pulled it from its holster as he ran.

Bone fumbled the thin Galaxy S7 in the air, tried to grab it, but it slipped from his fingers, tumbled end-over-end to the edge of the worn riser. It bounced all the way to the landing on the ground floor and broke apart, scattering the battery and the guts all over the landing. He stopped briefly to glance down to the bottom.

"Son-of-a-bitch!"

GAINESVILLE

Loraine picked up her radio mike and keyed it. "Kilo 12-55 to Ranger Bone…Come in Tiny."

"Ranger Bone, Kilo 12-55…What'd you got?"

"No answer. He always answers…Something's wrong. Meet you there…I'm 12 minutes away."

"Same here, Loraine, Tiny out."

"What has that hard-head gotten himself into? Supposed to wait for me before going in," Loraine muttered.

JOHNSON MILL

Stella ran from one side of the open third floor to the other. The huge building had been used to store pallets of processed flour. Windows lined the walls, but they didn't open. The mill was over a hundred years old, and had never been used for office or residences—it lacked emergency exits.

Rows of bare circular columns of reinforced concrete supported the upper floors.

Stella sprinted to the north side of the building. She looked out the windows into the moonlit darkness. The only thing she could see were several concrete grain silos that blocked the view inside the building.

Frantically, she came to the realization of her dire situation—there was no way out and no place to hide on that floor...

I-35 SOUTH OF ARDMORE, OKLAHOMA

Pat and Lisanne were twenty miles south of Ardmore, Oklahoma, heading toward Gainesville, still seventeen miles to the south across the Red River. Pat was at the wheel of the KTXP, Channel 14 news van.

Lisanne, in the passenger seat, glanced over at her camera operator. "Glad you were monitoring the scanner, Pat...We probably wouldn't have known about this until tomorrow."

Pat smiled. "Yes, ma'am, that's my job to keep on top of the police reports...among other things...Knew you were intrigued by this serial killer thing."

Lisanne nodded. "Yeah, don't have too many hot news events like the North Texas Butcher...It's even getting network play...They called and wanted our feed if anything broke...Do you know where that Johnson Mill is?"

"Oh, yes, ma'am…It's where that boy got killed back in the '50s…It's on Broadway Street, just west of Pecan Creek."

"How far?"

Pat glanced at her instrument panel. "'Bout 15 minutes…give or take."

"Judging from that police chatter we just listened to, something is going on and it's got the Rangers involved. Bet a dinner it's about the North Texas Butcher…Step on it.

"Pedal to the metal."

§§§

CHAPTER FOURTEEN

JOHNSON MILL

The sound of heavy footsteps coming up the stairs put Stella into a defensive mode. She spotted a small wooden crate that had formerly held nuts and bolts for the pallet racks that had been salvaged after the mill closed.

She put the knife in her teeth, picked up the crate and moved to the back edge of the stairwell.

Her kidnapper sprinted up the stairs, two at a time. His anger at her almost surpassed the pain in his groin. He breathed heavily, not used to such strenuous physical exertion.

GAINESVILLE

Loraine keyed her mic again. "Kilo 12-55 to dispatch…Lauri?"

"Dispatch. What's up Loraine?"

"Lauri, need all available units to the old Johnson Mill off Broadway. Bone is not responding…something's up."

"10-4, Loraine, I'm on it. Dispatch out…All available units, 10-46, all available units, 10-46, please respond. Officer needs assistance. Old Johnson Mill off Broadway. All units please respond."

Loraine hung her mic back on the side of her radio, popped her lights, hit her siren, and floorboarded her black plain detectives' unit east on the county road.

JOHNSON MILL

Stella hurled the crate down with all her might as the man left the second landing. It struck him on the top of his head and knocked the big man to his knees.

To her surprise and dismay, he let out a guttural yell, and turned to look up at her. His face was a hideous mask of rage. He got back to his feet and started up the stairs again.

"Oh, crap!" Stella sprinted to the closest two foot diameter pillar and tried to hide behind it. She had taken the knife from her teeth and held it beside her right thigh.

The man arrived on the third floor. "I've got you now," he hissed.

Stella held her breath as his footsteps drew closer and closer fearful he could hear her heart pounding because she could hear him panting. She said a silent prayer as she shook in fear. "Please…God. Let Jesus help me."

She took a deep breath, stepped out, drew her hand back, and threw the knife as hard as she could. It buried halfway up to the hilt in the man's upper left chest with an audible thunk—precisely splitting the two words on the left side of his work shirt—*Radio* and *Hut*.

He cried out, "Ahhh." And dropped to his knees, grabbed the knife and fell over, his eyes rolled back in his head, and after a few seconds, fluttered closed. A crimson stain began to soak his shirt...

GAINESVILLE

Captain St. John jumped up from his recliner in his den, strode to his adjacent office and picked up the mic on his home unit when he heard the all available units call.

His ten year old son, Damarcus, was watching TV laying in the floor. He turned and looked at his dad run into the office.

"Sierra 12 to dispatch."

"Dispatch, go ahead Captain."

"How many units do we have available, Lauri?"

"Only one…Sanchez. The rest are workin' that multi-car fatality pile-up on I-35."

"10-4, Lauri, log me in. I'm responding…and tell Sanchez to get his ass in gear."

"Yessir…10-4, Dispatch out."

St. John grabbed his side arm and jacket.

His wife, Sonjua, stepped in from the kitchen with a white dishtowel in her hands. "Got an emergency?"

St. John nodded. "If Bone's involved, hon, it always seems to turn into an emergency." He sprinted to the door.

JOHNSON MILL

Stella cautiously walked over to the body and stood there, looking down at him. "You sorry son of a…You got my address when I bought that toy Hummer for Bone."

She heard footsteps on the stairway a couple of floors down and turned to run away.

Suddenly the man's eyes snapped open, his hand shot out, grabbed her ankle, and he pulled her to the floor.

Stella screamed and kicked out with her free foot and caught the man full in the face. The crunching sound of cartilage in his nose breaking was followed by a gush of blood, and yet another scream of pain from the evil one.

"You bastard!" She kept kicking his face in rapid fire succession.

He let go of her ankle to cover his face.

Stella kicked away from him, and he began to moan. She jumped up and ran back toward the elevator shaft.

GAINESVILLE

Texas Ranger Tiny Bone roared north on Grand in his state unit, his lights were flashing, and siren wailing. He fishtailed around a corner, righted the car and sped on.

JOHNSON MILL

Bone heard her primal scream. "Stella...Hang in there, girl, I'm comin'...Bone's coming."

Lipschitz wobbled to his feet, straightened up, pulled the knife from his chest, and calmly wiped the bloody blade off on his pants. He stood there for a moment. His body swayed back and forth, plus his shirt was soaked in red from the knife wound, and also his crushed nose. He stuck the knife back into the scabbard on his belt and lurched after her...

GAINESVILLE

Loraine flew down the road, her lights also flashing, siren going. There was a look of deep concern on her face. She reached forward and turned her headlights on as twilight was rapidly covering the countryside from east to west.

JOHNSON MILL

Stella sprinted to the elevator shaft, leapt seven feet through the air, grabbed the rope that hung in the middle and began to rapidly climb again.

GAINESVILLE

Officer Jose Sanchez, lights and siren going, weaved around and through the traffic.

JOHNSON MILL

Bone hit the third floor landing—he saw Lipschitz moving toward the elevator shaft and charged like a linebacker. He tackled him—they both went down.

The fight was on. The butcher was as big, if not bigger, than Bone...not as tall, but he outweighed him by a good twenty pounds. He was getting the worst of the fight.

Bone hit him in the face, like a jack hammer with his left. The monstrous blows staggered him backward, but Lipschitz just shook his head and grinned at Bone.

He picked up a four foot length of a 2x4 and swung it like a baseball bat. He hit Bone across the chest and knocked him back toward the shaft. The cop stumbled over a 4x4 bolted to the concrete and tumbled into the opening.

The North Texas Butcher walked over to the edge and looked down. He could barely make out the inert figure of Bone lying motionless at the bottom....

GAINESVILLE

Captain St. John braked to a stop at the long bars down across the California Street crossing for a northbound train.

He banged on the steering wheel in frustration at the long train moving slowly through Gainesville.

"Dammit to hell! A one hundred car freight train...Son-of-a-green bitch!" He leaned his shaved pate forward and rested it at the top of the wheel.

JOHNSON MILL

Bone laid unconscious on a the same pile of burlap bags Stella had been on. Luckily, the thick pile of tow sacks had help cushion his fall.

Sixty feet above him, Stella steadily climbed hand-over-hand up the rope again. She reached the sixth floor and swung until she was able to release the rope and land on the top level.

Below, on the third floor, the North Texas Butcher looked up at her dark figure swinging over to land on the sixth. He turned and headed for the stairwell. He held one hand on the knife wound, trying to staunch the flow of blood from a lacerated thick pectoral muscle.

Lipschitz knew there was no way out, and this time, he was the one holding the knife. He forced himself to smile with his cut, swollen lips, exposed a tooth missing from his brief encounter with one of Gainesville's finest.

JOHNSON MILL

Stella frantically searched the sixth floor for a way out or something to fight with—there was no way out. She found a four foot length of one and three-eights plumbing pipe, picked it up, crouched beside the stairwell wall, and waited as she heard footsteps coming up the stairs. In the distance she could hear sirens...

The clerk reached the sixth floor. He stepped on the landing and tried to survey the darkness. The area was vacant, except for the concrete support columns.

Stella stood in the shadows behind the short protective wall beside the stairwell, waiting with her length of pipe.

Lipschitz stepped out on to the floor. Stella swung the four foot length of pipe. She connected with the back of the big man's head with a thud.

The killer fell forward on his face. Not waiting to check out the damage, this time, Stella headed down the stairway.

Lipschitz pulled himself to his knees, and then staggered to his feet...

§§§

CHAPTER FIFTEEN

GAINESVILLE

The last car of the train had cleared the crossing and the arms finally went up. St. John put his car in gear, floored it and laid two longs strips of rubber, bouncing across the tracks.

JOHNSON MILL

Stella could hear heavy steps coming down the stairway behind her. She moved out of the stairway on the bottom floor and could see the large number of vehicles parked in the huge open area and sprinted toward them.

The killer exited the stairway behind her, saw Stella just as she went around the nearest vehicle, and he stalked toward her like the great white shark in *Jaws*.

Stella crouched behind the car to look back toward the stairway. She saw the butcher as he moved directly toward her.

"Damn, is this guy for real?" she muttered.

She spun, slid, and then scrambled under a restored dark green 1941 Plymouth pickup—the man was almost on her.

Stella crawled further under the truck when Lipschitz grabbed for the back of her heel. His bloody hand slipped off her foot as she scrambled out the other side.

She quickly opened the door of the next car, a turquoise and white 1955 Chevrolet Bel Air two door hardtop, crawled in, and scrunched down in the seat...

Loraine pulled in and slid to a stop next to Bone's Thing. Sanchez was right behind her and he was followed immediately by Captain St. John.

They all exited their vehicles about the same time.

St. John immediately took charge. "What'd we got?"

Loraine looked at him. "Don't know, Captain, we just got here, all we have is Bone's Thing here and that white Ford van."

"Let's split up and cover all exits..."

Lipschitz was still on his knees looking under the pickup trying to see Stella's feet—nothing. He raised back up and walked around to the other side.

Stella peeked through the bottom edge of the glass just enough to see out the driver's window and saw him coming around. She put her hand on the door handle.

He bent over to look under the car. Stella flipped the handle and kicked the door as hard as she could with both feet, slamming him in the head. He was knocked backwards.

Stella scooted out the passenger door and jumped up on top of a 1955 Ford Woody Station Wagon.

Lipschitz got to his feet, headed around to the other side, saw Stella jump up on top of the wagon and moved once more toward her.

He reached out to grab her leg. Stella executed a text book spin kick to the side of his head directly on his ear, and then did a back flip over his head. Her landing on the floor was perfect, and she sprinted back toward the stairway.

Stella charged up the stairs with the killer hot on her heels. She reached the fourth floor, turned and ran toward the elevator shaft, leapt in the air, grabbing the rope like Tarzan, and started climbing down.

The man reached the fourth floor behind her and moved over to the elevator shaft. He saw Stella climbing down, glanced around, and spied a five foot piece of rebar.

He picked it up, bent a hook in one end with his bare hands, leaned forward, reached out with the rebar, hooked the rope, and pulled it to him. He took his knife from the scabbard, and started cutting the inch and a half thick hemp.

Stella looked up, loosened her grip a little, and slid down as fast as she could. The cords of the rope began to unravel and then parted.

Stella fell the last ten feet to the bottom of the shaft. She landed next to the still unconscious Bone...

Tiny slid into the parking area beside the other vehicles already there. He jumped out of his vehicle, gun in hand.

"Anybody know anything?'

"We just got here too, Ranger," said St. John.

Stella shook Bone's shoulder. "Bone! Bone! Wake up! Please wake up."

She looked up, saw the dim image of the silhouetted giant of a man looking down at her in the murky moonlit darkness. She glanced back to

Bone, saw his S&W 500 still in its holster. She grabbed it and with a two-handed grip, rolled onto her back and cranked off two rounds, center mass, into the man's chest. The roar was deafening in the confined area…

"Holy Crap! That's Bone's hand cannon." Tiny bolted for the door closest to his brother's car. "Cover me!" he called back over his shoulder. "St. John, you and Sanchez take the side. Go, go, go!…Loraine, you're with me."

She was already only two steps behind him.

St. John keyed his handheld radio. "Shots fired, shots fired. Officer involved shooting at the old Johnson Mill."

The van with the TV crew from Ardmore braked to a stop fifteen feet away.

The captain shook his head. "Oh, Jesus…Not now, Lord…Not now."

Lipschtiz staggered, with fist sized chunks of his back missing. He screamed once again and pointed an accusing finger down at Stella.

She thumbed the hammer back on the 500 and squeezed the trigger a third time. Her shot hit the butcher at the bridge of his nose.

The top of his head exploded in a gory mist with a shower of blood and brain matter covering a twenty foot circle. The monster's knees buckled and his body—as if in slow motion—leaned over and plummeted down the shaft followed by chunks of skull and a veritable rain of more blood.

Stella was certain he would land on top of her. She screamed…

Lisanne and Pat bailed out of their van and quickly opened the side door.

Lisanne reached in and grabbed her wireless mic the first thing. "Pat, quick, get the gear, this is our chance."

"Yes, ma'am." She unbuckled her steadycam, removed it from the van and checked the battery.

St. John looked back over his shoulder. "Stay back! You people stay back!"

Lisanne grinned and replied sotto, "Or not."

They immediately followed St. John and Sanchez to the side entrance.

Tiny and Loraine entered the office of the feed mill, swat style. T-Bone took the right side, Loraine the left. Weapons at the ready as they spun through the door and separated to each side.

St. John and Sanchez went into the entrance on the south side of the mill in the same manner as Tiny and Loraine.

Stella got to her feet and wiped the blood spray from her eyes and pointed the 500 at the motionless Lipschitz. She saw that the entire back half of his head had been blown off.

"Shake that off, asshole."

Bone groaned, rolled over, sat up, shook his head, looked at the body of the killer, and then up at Stella.

"Thought I was supposed to be rescuing you, Little Bit."

"You were taking a nap."

His trademark grin spread across his face. "Nap, my ass…How'd you do this?"

She returned the smile and shrugged. "Stella happens."

Bone got to his feet, grabbed Stella, and pulled her close in a tender embrace. "Oh, Baby, I was so scared."

She leaned back and craned her neck so she could look up at his face. There were rivulets of tears running down the big man's face.

"You? I thought you never got scared."

"Not so, honey, not so…I was scared to death we might have lost you…I couldn't bear it…I just couldn't."

"Oh, Bone…thank you." She handed the pistol back to him. "Really like your .50 cal. and I'm so glad you taught me how to shoot it."

Bone holstered the weapon. "Yeah, me too…When you have to shoot somebody…they stay shot." He looked at her standing there in the semi darkness wearing just panties and bra. " Cute outfit, Little Bit…but, would you like some cover?"

"You think?"

Bone took off his jacket and helped Stella into it.

She looked at the sleeves that went way past her hands. "Just a tad big an' not my color...but it'll do. I could make a blanket out of this thing...Thanks."

A blinding bright light hit Stella and Bone from Loraine's flashlight as she and Tiny arrived down the stairs...weapons still drawn.

"Ya'll all right?" asked T-Bone.

"Are now," replied Bone.

Loraine raised her head and shouted up the shaft. "Captain! They're here at the bottom of the elevator shaft." She looked at Bone and Stella. "Damn, looks like you two need to go through a car wash...You're going to start stinking PDQ."

Lisanne heard Loraine, she turned to her camera girl. "This way, Pat...Turn on the camera and the lights."

"Camera is rolling...We have sound."

Pat followed Lisanne with the camera as she moved rapidly across the floor toward the stairway to the basement only a few feet behind St. John.

186

RECIPE FOR MURDER

The Captain and Sanchez arrived at the basement followed immediately by Lisanne and Pat.

St. John turned to the reporter. "Thought I told you to stay back."

"Oh! Is that what you said?"

St. John rolled his eyes.

Pat moved forward and focused in on Bone and Stella. She tilted the camera down to the killer's face. Her eyes widened.

Captain St. John reached over and put his hand over the lens. "Out, out, out!"

"Just doing my job, sir…Who is he?"

"None of your damn business, now get out!"

"Pat, on me." She paused for a beat. "This is Lisanne Miller with a Channel 14 live update from Gainesville, Texas…In the apparent culmination of the massive man hunt for the serial killer that has been terrorizing women…known as the North Texas Butcher…abducted Officer Stella Johnson has been rescued by Gainesville police officers, unharmed, after a bloody gun battle resulting in the death of the suspected killer."

Lisanne moved her mic toward Bone. "Detective Bone…"

"Well, Lisanne, you know I don't really have a little…"

She gasped, covered the top of her mic with her hand when she remembered a past interview with Bone, and swung the mic over to Captain St. John.

"Uh, Captain St. John, do you have a statement?"

He put his arm around Stella's shoulders under Bone's massive coat. "I'll have a full statement in the morning, Lisanne…Right now, I'm just happy that my officer is safe."

§§§

CHAPTER SIXTEEN

JOHNSON MILL

Wanda Stanton drove into the parking area to add her flashing lights to the melee. Peach Presley was riding with her.

Officers Newman and his partner, Sandra Parker, also parked in the lot as they came to assist after working the fatality crash on the interstate.

Peach jumped out and ran inside the front of the building. She immediately saw the camera lights of Channel 14 and headed toward them.

She rushed up to Stella, her best friend, and wrapped her in a hug. "Oh, sweet pea, are you okay?" Peach stepped back a little and looked at the blood and gore all over her and on Bone's coat. "Baby, you look like you been rode hard an' put away wet…an' smell even worse."

"Thanks, Peach…I'm fine, a little sore, an' nothin' else a good hot shower won't take care of."

"Bless your heart, you won't believe what's in your hair."

"Think I know." Stella turned to Bone. "I'll have your coat cleaned an' get it back to you."

The big man looked at the blood and brain matter that had rained down on it. "Think you can just burn it, Little Bit. Don't believe they can get all that crud out of there with Bab-O."

"Got a point."

Stanton walked up to St. John. "Captain, that white Ford van has Stella's clothes in it...the clothes she wore at the Governor's Lounge."

"Bag 'em for evidence, Stanton."

"Yes, sir...Thought as much. Sorry Stella."

"Understand...Procedure. Wondered what he did with them. Woke up down in that basement in just bra an' panties."

Bone held up her necklace with the small .22. "Found this over there by the door on a tow sack." He pointed. "Must have fallen off when he carried you in and down to the basement. Apparently he removed your clothes down there, and then put them in his van when he left after dumping you."

St. John turned to Peach. "Presley, go over that van with a fine tooth comb...DNA, hairs...everything."

The 5'10" forensics technician looked down at the shorter captain. "Oh, honey, you know this isn't my first brush arbor meetin'...Have it towed in to our compound before you can say scat."

Newman held up an iPhone in a plastic baggie. "Found this in the van, too."

"Give it to Peach. No telling what we'll find on it," offered Bone.

"I'll take care of it, buttercup." Peach took the bag from the officer.

"Bone…"

"I know, Cap'n, check the building from A to Z…Thinking that the four vics weren't all there were?"

St. John looked up. "Exactly."

Lisanne never stopped her camera from rolling as she and Pat stood off to the side. A Cooke County EMS ambulance rolled up and pulled to a stop.

Once it parked, two young men in matching powder blue Emergency Medical Technician shirts and wind breakers got out and walked to the back of the unit.

With the rear doors held wide open, they removed the gurney and flipped a lever to allow the wheels and undercarriage to fall free. The med techs rolled it to the south door of the building, but stopped and looked at Bone.

"Sorry, Cap'n. Looks like the body snatchers are waitin' to be escorted into the crime scene. Catch you later."

"Carry on, diamond head. See you tomorrow."

St. John turned and walked to one of the nearest patrol units as Bone and the EMS crew disappeared into the mill.

Pat stopped filming and gave a *cut* sign to Lisanne, basically pulling a flat hand across her throat. She motioned for the brunette media star to come closer.

"Why'd you stop?"

Pat grinned. "Thought you might want to give the folks a major scoop...one that will insure the networks pick up this feed tonight."

Lisanne laughed. "You know I'd raffle off my first born for a big one...What are you holding back?"

It was Pat's turn to laugh. She looked around and made sure no one was eavesdropping. "I know the name of the North Texas Butcher."

Lisanne's mouth dropped. "Who? How?...You certain?"

Pat nodded. "He was in my senior class at Denton High School...Name's Bernie Lipschitz."

"You're absolutely positive? I can't be wrong on this."

"Bernie sat across from me in science class and was in my home room, too...Never forget that face, well, at least what's left of it…Bernie was huge but didn't want to play football for some reason."

"If the networks pick it up, there'll be a bonus for you." Lisanne looked back over her shoulder. "Be ready…when they bring him out, I want a wide shot with the gurney starting over my left shoulder as I announce the scoop. Then zoom in on the body as they roll out on the right side. Keep it on him until they close the door and then back to me for a wrap-up."

"Have I ever let you down?" Pat held up her hand for a high five.

GAINESVILLE

Bone, Loraine and Stella were headed down the street toward Stella's house to take her home when a call crackled over the radio.

"All units, B and E in progress, 106 West Curtis, nearest unit respond."

Bone grabbed his radio mic. "Kilo 12-36, Lauridarlin', I'm two blocks away…I'll take it."

"Didn't know you were on duty, Bone."

"Not, Lauridarlin'. Taking Stella home. Just close to 106 West Curtis. Send a uniform back up...Wanda should be free by now."

"10-4, Bone. Stanton's just leavin' the mill. She can be there in five."

"Copy that...Bone out."

By the time the radio conversation with dispatch was over and he had hung up his mic, the Thing braked to a stop at 106 West Curtis.

Bone grabbed his extra .50 cal from his shooting bag as he had left his regular one with the captain for Stella's Grand Jury hearing on the shooting they knew would be forthcoming.

He, Loraine, and Stella exited the vehicle. Stella was still wearing Bone's jacket and carried Loraine's backup.

"Loraine, you take the back, Stella you're with me."

Loraine, weapon at the tactical position, moved toward the back. Bone, and Stella, their weapons also at the tactical, stepped to the front door.

The door opened and a gray-haired, little old lady came out. "Officers, officers, quick, around back. There's a man stuck in my pet door."

Bone and Stella sprinted toward the back.

"Did she say what I thought she said?" asked Stella as they ran.

"Sounded like it."

They rounded the corner to find Loraine, doubled over in laughter, looking at a teenager's legs, butt, and hands sticking out of a very small pet door at the bottom of the back door—he was yelling.

"Help! Help! Somebody help me! This dog is eatin' me alive!"

Bone walked up, grabbed the door knob, and opened it, dragging the boy inside. The little old lady inside had a broom—a small fox terrier was busy snapping and barking at the man's head.

The woman was swatting at the teenager with the business end of the broom and encouraging her dog.

"Get 'em Brutus, get 'em."

The tiny dog worried at one of the teen's ears.

"Ow, Ow, hey, hey, help!"

Loraine grinned. "Think you can call off your guard dog, Ma'am."

"All right, Brutus, that's enough…Sit."

The little dog growled once more at the boy and sat down two inches from his face, his upper lip curled up in a snarl.

"Ma'am, do you have any dish washing liquid?"

She looked at Stella. "Young lady why are you wearin' that nasty coat?"

"Long story, Ma'am…Now, 'bout that soap."

"Why, yes, of course."

"Please get it for us."

Bone and Loraine were doing their best not to burst out laughing.

The lady stepped over to her kitchen sink, took a bottle of liquid soap from the counter and brought it to Stella.

She liberally wet the boy's butt and arms, which were wedged in the door.

Stella smiled. "Just like pullin' a calf."

Officer Wanda Stanton and Peach walked around the corner and saw the teenager stuck in the pet door.

Peach shook her head. "My goodness gracious, I do declare…He must be dumber'n a doorknob."

Wanda grinned and looked at Loriane. "This is candid camera, right?"

"We didn't check for cameras, Wanda."

"Loraine, you and Peach hold the door. Wanda, you get on the other side and push from his head...Little Bit, you just watch. Those hands of yours look a bit raw."

Stella nodded as Bone picked up the boy's feet, leaned back and pulled him back out of the door. He slid easily after being lubricated by the soap.

Bone continued to lift until the boy was completely out of the pet door and upside down—his ankles were still held by Bone.

Wanda knelt down beside the teenager's face. One of his ears was bleeding from Brutus' attack.

"Did your Mama have any children that lived?..." She pulled him to his feet after Bone laid him down and snapped the cuffs on him. "You have the right to remain stupid..."

Stella watched Wanda and Peach escort the teen around the corner to her unit parked out front and shook her head. "Thought I'd seen most everything till tonight."

Bone grinned. "Oh, there's a lot more crazies out there yet, Little Bit...Ought to watch that TV show, "*Stupid Things Criminals Do*."

BONE RANCH

Bone and Padrino sat on the porch having before bed drinks.

"So, you got the killer?" asked Padrino.

"It would seem...Stella blew him to hell and gone with my .50."

"I know you, Bone...Somethin's bothering you."

"Yeah, something's not right...Don't know what it is...yet." Bone took a sip of his Patron tequila and savored the smooth taste. "But there is one thing I hate about tonight."

"That would be?"

"Broke my phone...Got no way to contact Lucy now." He reached into the side pocket of his BDUs, took out a handful of parts and held them in his hand to show Padrino.

"Is she nearby?"

"She's at their permanent watcher observation station at Lagrangian Point Two."

"Ah, yes, one of the five points of gravitational equilibrium around Earth's orbit, named after the Italian-French mathematician Joseph Louis Lagrange in 1772."

"Yeah, him…The Anunnaki have had someone stationed there for millennia…Lucy gave me this…Humpty Dumpty had a great…"

The parts in his hand shimmered briefly and a brand new Galaxy S7 appeared where the loose parts had been.

The air in front of them also shimmered and Lucy, sans her helmet with the big black almond eye-like visor that went with her gray one-piece formfitting suit, appeared. Tyrin jumped up, wagged his tail, danced on his front feet, and woofed at her hologram.

"Hello, Tyrin, how's my boy?"

He woofed again.

"How did you know, Lucy?" asked Bone.

"My dear Bone, you should know better than to ask, but when your signal ceased to exist, I knew your phone had been destroyed…So, that's a new one, identical with the old, but with all upgraded apps."

"Way cool."

"How have you been, my Sky Queen?" Padrino smiled at the diminutive Anunnaki.

She smiled back. "I've told you, Padrino, that title wasn't necessary.

"Old habits."

Bone looked down at his new phone, and then back at her. "When will we see you again...in the flesh?"

"Maybe sooner than you think." She grinned knowingly.

The air shimmered again and her image disappeared.

"That always gives me the heebie-jeebies when she does that," said Bone.

"Well, least you have a new phone."

Bone pressed the center button at the bottom—the screen came to life. He swiped his thumb across the glass.

There in the upper right hand corner was the tiny icon of the gray alien face he could use to contact Lucy out at Lagrangian Point Two.

§§§

CHAPTER SEVENTEEN

GAINESVILLE PD

Much of the perpetrator's white van lay about the floor of the PD compound garage in pieces. Peach knelt at the open side with a high power light in her right hand and powerful magnifying goggles over her eyes.

She carefully panned the light over the carpeted interior previously sprayed evenly with luminol, the chemical compound spray that causes the ferrous molecules in hemoglobin, fecal matter, and to a lesser degree, urine, to glow a bright blue.

"Kiss my grits." Peach marked the several different stains showing up in the light and took multiple photographs since the glow would only last thirty seconds or so. "Dang sure more than four different spots…least six." She habitually muttered to herself as she worked.

She had donned a white plastic gown and booties, along with surgical gloves. Peach climbed inside from the end of the van—the doors already removed. She panned the light around scanning for aberrant fibers and hair over the entire length of the van.

Peach carefully picked up each hair or fiber and put them into individual plastic bags.

Bone, Tiny Bone, and Loraine entered St. John's office and took a seat. The rather small area was filled to capacity.

"Boss, looks like you need bigger digs." Bone grinned. "Anderson's office is a lot larger."

"No doubt, but he should be back in a few days. Hear he still has a little nausea."

Detective Bone pressed his knees together. "And some major bruising to Mister Happy."

St. John shook his head. "All thanks to you and that .500 Smith."

The big man shrugged. "You know what they say...'Bone happens', or in this case, 'Stella happened'."

"All in all, I suppose we should be grateful that Stella could get her hands on it. Don't think a nine millimeter would have fazed that big son of a bitch."

T-Bone laughed. "Gotta agree. If my little big brother couldn't clean his clock, he was one tough hombre."

"I'd taken him, but I tripped."

"Sure you would, Darrell."

St. John raised his hand. "Enough of that...why I called you in was to ask what your investigation is doing to wrap this case up...nice and tidy."

Loraine spoke first, "We want to look at all the recent missing person files in the three county..."

Just then, the flat screen TV on the captain's wall, displayed a *Breaking News* banner. The full time news network—always on at a low volume—displayed a crawler at the bottom on the screen. *North Texas Butcher identified*.

Bone's ears picked up on a familiar voice.

"Hello, I'm Lisanne Miller with this exclusive bit of information...Eyewitness news reports that the serial killer known as the North Texas Butcher, who was killed late last night by Gainesville police, has been positively identified as one Bernie Lipschitz, originally from Denton Texas."

Footage from last night rolled across the screen as Lisanne talked, including Lipschitz's face down in the basement, and his high school picture. "He graduated from high school there fifteen years ago. Classmates remember him as a large and powerful man who had few friends. There are four known victims attributed to the Butcher...so far..."

"Dammit to hell! Who gave her that information?" St. John shot to his feet, stomped around in a tight circle, stopped, and looked accusingly at the three seated across the room.

"Boss, you know better than that." Bone chuckled. "Think I pretty well broke 'em from suckin' eggs the first time they tried to interview me."

Loraine shook her head. "Never said a word to the woman."

"Hey, Captain, I know better than to release sensitive information. Maybe she got it from the EMS crew."

"No way, T-Bone. She was recording live as they wheeled the DB out of the building. Needless to say, a leak in this department has pissed me off in a major way." Veins on the captain's forehead began to bulge.

"Calm down, Cap'n...Breathe, just breathe. We'll get it figured out. None of us did it, but somebody knew something we didn't."

"Back to the main reason I called ya'll in. Who's on first?"

Bone thumbed toward the south end of the police complex. "Peach has the killer's van inside the inspection bay in the garage doin' her CSI thing. We three will head out and do the same in the mill and at his residence. He lived in a trailer park...Might take a while."

"I'd say so." St. John pointed at Bone. "While you're at it...in your spare time...do a little actual detective work and find out where that reporter got her info...Think you can do that for me?"

Bone grinned as he pulled out his phone. "Don't know. My dance card is kinda full." He slid his finger across the face, opening a window. The big guy tapped a single icon and spoke softly. "Lisanne Miller." It began ringing. He put it on speaker.

She picked it up on the second ring. "Detective Bone. Imagine hearing from you."

"Hey, Pretty Lady. Caught your scoop on network news. Nicely done."

"Thank you Mister Bone. Appreciate the compliment."

"We know none of us leaked his ID to you...was wonderin'...Where did you go to high school?"

"Dang it, Bone. Guess that's why you make such a great detective...You are so, so close. But I graduated from high school in Lone Oak."

"So, that would mean your camera gal is from Denton."

There was silence on the other end as Lisanne pondered her response.

Bone's grin widened. "No need to answer that, sweet pea. I'll never make you give up your sources. First Amendment is right up there with the Second in my book."

"I'm not at liberty to divulge that information, anyway, Detective."

"Just call me Bone, Lisanne…We go way back, we do. Besides, we'll pick her senior picture out of the annual when we check. Think you call her Pat…that right?"

Lisanne let out a long sigh. "You are a quick one. Remind me never to get on your wrong side."

Bone laughed. "Never. Tell you what…Next time you come across the Red River, call me. Maybe I can make you dinner out at the ranch. You a seafood girl? Italian?…I do it all."

Loraine shot him a look.

"Love Italian… Just a simple dinner, no strings, right?"

"No strings. Just one professional to another. I really respect your work…Seriously. Sorry, but the captain is on my butt to get some cop work done today…Laterbye."

Bone closed the call. "Okay, boss you can let your blood pressure drop down below two hundred." He glanced at Loraine as she raised a single eyebrow. "Taking notes, Pard?"

St. John shook his head. "Bone you are so full of crap. She fell for it hook, line, and sinker. Cannot believe she basically gave up her camera gal that easy."

"Not my first rodeo, is it now?...Come on kiddies Let the nice man do his play acting chief stuff while we go to the salt mines."

They got to their feet and headed down the hall. Tiny elbowed Bone. "Slick move, bro. She's kinda hot, too."

Loraine shot T-Bone a withering glance.

Peach, with multitudinous photos, plastic bags of fibers and hairs, and vials of blood samples extracted from the carpet with distilled water, walked into her lab inside the PD.

She turned on her audio system and selected her George Strait collection. Strains of his signature music soon filled Peach's inner sanctum.

She laid all the items in a regular order on a long work table and started working on the blood samples first to discern the type and start the process for DNA.

Once they were all in her multiple sample centrifuge, she extracted the hair samples and mounted them on individual slides for her powerful microscope.

The microscope was electronically linked to her computer and monitor so she could enlarge and display the view on the screen and save the results on an 8 TB external hard drive storage unit.

She plugged her camera into the external drive and downloaded all the pictures.

Peach picked up her remote and displayed each hair sample on the monitor. "Well, butter my butt an' call me a biscuit."

She picked up her cell, opened it and punched a speed dial number. The other end picked up on the second ring.

"Bone, speak now or forever hold it."

"It's Peach, get down to my lab...Now."

The three officers walked out of the Crime Investigators Unit and entered Peach's Forensics Lab.

"What's up, girl?" Bone looked at the Georgia peach.

She pointed at her big monitor and clicked a button on her remote.

"What do you see, buttercup?"

Bone squinted. "Uh, kind of a funny railroad track?"

"Close. Bless your heart, Bone…Awallago…"

"Do what?"

Peach looked at him and cocked her head. "Awallago, I…"

"What the hell's an awallago?"

Tiny Bone burst out laughing. "Awallago, Bone, don't you know nothin'?…That's southern for a while ago."

He looked at his brother. "You jest."

Peach glared at him. "Honey, you're so precious, I'm…"

Tiny elbowed him. "Brother, when a southern woman uses 'honey' and 'precious' in the same sentence…it's fixin' to hit the fan."

Bone held up both hands. "Sorry, Peach, didn't know. I apologize."

"Well, ignorance sometimes can't be helped…Ya'll ready for this?"

"Go for it girl," said Loraine.

"This is gonna knock your hat in the creek...Those are hairs from whats his names' van...There are seven different ones an' one of 'em's his."

"So you're saying there were six vics?" Loraine turned and looked at her.

"Hot damn, you're good, Loraine." She grinned and batted her eyelashes. "Oh, thank the Lord, thought I was talkin' to fence posts."

§§§

CHAPTER EIGHTEEN

JOHNSON MILL

Bone, with Loraine, pulled into the south parking lot of the mill. T-Bone drove in and parked beside him in his state unit.

Bone hit the release for the trunk, which is in the front of the rear engine Thing, got out, and opened his investigation bag. From a side pocket, he took a pair of extra large powder blue latex gloves and carefully slipped them on.

Bone grabbed his CSI kit from the trunk. "Pard, bring a couple of those black plastic bags out from under the seat, please."

"Feeling optimistic are you?" Loraine bent over and counted out two from the box.

"Well, I know at least one vic was kept here. Time will tell what else we find."

He set the bag down in front of the entrance door. Bone slipped his index finger into a metal ring barely visible in his right front pants pocket. In one a quick motion, he dragged out an Italian made Fox Karambit knife.

A hook made into the back of the wicked curved blade caught on the pocket seam and snapped the blade out into a locked position. The big man punched at the yellow tape emblazoned with the words *POLICE CRIME SCENE DO NOT CROSS* .

The tape fluttered to the ground.

"You know that knife always scares the hell out of me." Loraine shivered.

"Seriously? It's just a tool." Bone pressed the release, folded it back up and tucked it into his jeans.

T-Bone laughed. "He always says that. Sucker is sharp, grant you that...even if it is somewhat massive overkill."

"Overkill? Your brother doesn't know what that word means...Look at his duty weapon." She chuckled.

"Ya'll can yuck it up all day long, kiddies...Have my way of doing things and don't fancy myself changin'." He shot a fake smile to his partner and opened the door. "Ladies first. Wasn't even locked."

Inside, the trio had to use their tac lights, as the building had no electrical power.

"Let's start in the basement," Bone suggested. "We know that he kept Stella there."

T-Bone nodded. "Sounds reasonable. Expect we can do the upper floors faster while there's still plenty of daylight."

"They are pretty open from what I recall." Bone led them to the stairway to the underground room.

Loraine broke out the spray bottles of Luminol.

"Pard, I'm not sure that's a great idea. When Stella triple tapped her kidnapper, his melon covered most of the room as well as us."

T-Bone nodded. "Was thinking we might bag the top eight or ten tow sacks and let the lab check them for DNA and hair...Bet there's stray cat and rat hair on 'em as well."

Bone pondered the situation for a second. "See what you mean. Didn't realize how lucky I was until I saw how thick these sacks piled up on each other were." He looked up at the third floor. "Damn...hell of a fall."

Tiny agreed. "Got that right...God was looking out for you."

"Uh-huh...Hold on, ya'll. Got an idea. Be real quiet for a minute. Wanna try somethin'."

Bone removed his hat and knelt down on one knee. He placed his gloved hand on top of the pile of filthy burlap bags. He took in a deep breath, let it out slowly as he closed his eyes.

Tiny looked over at Loraine. His face conveyed the question. "What the hell is he doin'?"

She brought her index finger to her lips and then made a hand signal for *stop* followed by *okay*.

RECIPE FOR MURDER

The ranger nodded as his older brother's head moved as if he was looking around the room.

In Bone's vision, *Stella appeared, lying motionless in the center of the room, and tied up with silver duct tape. The image of Stella shimmered and faded one of a woman with henna hair took her place. A few seconds later, she vanished and a redhead appeared. Her bra was burgundy and her matching panties were cut high on the sides.*

The second victim became invisible only to be replaced by a mulatto woman with long dark hair. She was lying on her side and her fingernail polish appeared to be a distinct color—like robin's egg blue.

Suddenly the visions stopped. Bone's eyes fluttered open.

"You okay, bud?" Tiny stepped closer and helped him to his feet.

"Yeah, sure…Just a little woozy."

"Mind telling me what that was all about?"

Bone grinned. "Lucy taught me that I was an empath…I can see things after they happen."

T-Bone shook his head. "Just when I thought I knew all your BS lines…"

"No, he's serious. It's real." Loraine stepped closer to her partner. "Tell us what you saw."

"I saw three victims. Stella, the gal from northern Cooke County, and a redhead that didn't show up in the four known murder cases."

Tiny was still skeptical. "None of that is admissible in court, you know. Some shrink would say that your subconscious simply replayed the images of the victims."

"You don't have to believe it T...But I bet you a sixpack I can pick out the redhead from a list of missing persons...She was a looker."

"You're on. Heinekens for me if you're full of it...Now, who the hell is Lucy?"

"Tell you over a beer."

GAINESVILLE PD

Stella sat in the Crime Investigation Unit at Loraine's desk. She had refused to stay home to recuperate, and the captain assigned her desk duty for the time being.

St. John gave her a research assignment on Bernie Lipschitz. "Run the perp's bank records an' after you do the last two years on that, you can start on his phone…save Bone an' them a lot of time an' leg work…or finger work…plus good experience for you. Don't figure you plan on being a patrol cop all your life."

She looked up at him from under her brow. "You say so. But, I'd rather…"

He held up his hand. "Don't want to hear it." He turned on his heel and strode out of the room.

JOHNSON MILL

Once the room was photographed and the empty grain sacks tagged and collected, the trio took to the stairs and spread out on the top floor.

They found footprints of Bernie chasing Stella, but nothing else of use.

A cold north wind whistled through the broken windows as they descended and repeated the search below.

When they made it down to the third floor, Bone stared at the ten foot long 4x4 bolted to the floor near the elevator shaft. "So that's what tripped me." He peeked over the edge and whistled slowly. *Damn long way down.*

Loraine chuckled. "It's not the fall that gets you…"

He shot her a hard look. "Yeah, yeah, I know…The sudden stop at the bottom…Funny, Double D…Real funny."

Tiny grinned. "Don't forget what I said about bein' your best man."

"Put a sock in, bro…You're fantasizing again…Cold day in hell."

"Sure. Anythin' you say, Darrell…Hey, gettin' close to lunch time. Any good cafeteria's around here?"

"Slim pickin's I'm afraid. Guess I like my own cooking too much…Hold on, speaking of cafeterias…now that you mention it, Pard, do you remember that blueprint of the first floor?"

Loraine glanced back at Bone. "Sure, what about it?"

"The employee cafeteria? Not very big, and it's east, past all those cars…What's your point?…It's closed."

She glared at him.

"My point is there was no evidence of frequent use of the top floors. No blood from the vics in the basement or office…"

"Ah!…What if he strangled them down there, and *then* took the bodies to the cafeteria for the slice and dice?"

"Hey…Good thinkin', Pard. What say we sashay that way and give it a looksee?"

T-Bone nodded. "Works for me."

GAINESVILLE PD

Stella scrolled the screen with Lipschitz's bank records. "Hmm, interestin'." She jotted down some notes in her notebook. "Bone's gonna like this…Now for the phone."

JOHNSON MILL

Inside the cafeteria was a sixty plus year old menu and price list on the wall in the barren room where the employees used to eat. It was covered with dust, just like the floor, walls, and basically everything else in the defunct mill.

Tiny took several pictures of the footprints in the dust. "At least two different people…One huge set, at least a size thirteen and another much smaller…maybe an eight or nine."

Bone took a couple pictures himself. "No bare feet. Wager the killer carried the vics in here. Those show a lot of weight."

"They all lead to and from the kitchen area." Loraine pointed at the doorway with galley style kitchen.

T-Bone stopped short of the entry door to the cafeteria. "Ya'll want to make casts of the footprints?"

"Negatory, good buddy. High def digital pics can tell us 'bout everything we need to know about the foot wear. I'll drop a ruler beside the smaller prints, 'cause I'll guarandamntee you the larger ones are from Bernie."

Loraine entered the dining room. "Want to see what's behind that serving counter." She pointed at the low wall.

All the metal warming trays, racks, and tiny Sterno cans were long gone.

Tiny glanced at the menu. "Holy moly…Can't imagine buying a blue plate special lunch for seventy five cents." He took a picture for his Facebook page.

"How 'bout a chicken fried steak, mashed potatoes, salad, and iced tea for ninety cents?" Bone chuckled.

Loraine forged ahead and stuck her head inside the kitchen. "Guys, you gotta see this."

Bone looked over. "Whatcha got?"

"A stainless steel prep table, mop bucket, and wooden handled mop...and a linoleum floor with no dust on it."

"Say what?" Tiny moved to the doorway and glanced in. "Now we can break out the Luminol. Bet money we get a hit on the floor and the bucket...Might even get some DNA."

Bone eased in beside his brother. "All the refrigerators, stoves, and sinks were hauled off for salvage." He saw the four rusty bolts and nuts on each pad at the base of table legs and pointed. "Thinkin' they didn't want to spend the effort to break those rusty suckers loose."

Tiny took several wide shots, as did Loraine. "Bro, can you do that empath vision thing again in this room?

Bone shook his head. "Uh-uh…Doesn't work that way with dead people. Gotta have a life force to create an aura that permeates the area. It lasts for several days then slowly dissipates. The stronger the fear and adrenaline was in the person, the stronger the aura."

Loraine dug out two bottles of Luminol and a battery powered black light from her kit. She handed one to Bone.

"Right around the table and in the corners next to the wall. Anywhere else?"

"Maybe they didn't do a great job on the table itself. There's no runnin' water, so they had to bring it in with 'em."

"Okay, I'll buy that. Bet they were real careful to try to keep it off their shoes…Probably had aprons, or gowns, too."

T-Bone watched as his compatriots did their thing. The trio doused their flashlights and were rewarded with a massive glow from the Luminol on the table and floor under the ultraviolet beam.

"Bingo."

Bone slowly looked around as Loraine bathed the room with her device. "They always think they cleaned up really well, but the truth will come to light."

Ouside, in the parking lot, Bone came up with an idea. "Why don't we stash all these evidence bags in T-Bone's trunk and ride together over to Bernie's trailer house?…Only a couple miles."

"If we can stop for something to eat. I'm still a growing boy."

Loraine shook her head.

"How 'bout barbecue? There's a place up on Highway 82 on the way."

"Sign me up." Tiny hit the remote on his sedan to open the trunk.

With everything stowed away, the three climbed into the Thing. Loraine graciously let Tiny sit up front as the leg room in the back was way too tight for a 6'11" guy.

Bone glanced up at the building before he turned the ignition key. Movement caught his eye. A small boy in a red and blue baseball team shirt waved down at them from the second floor.

Bone waved back. Loraine looked up and waved as well.

Tiny looked at Bone. "What are you doing now?"

"Just waving at some kid in a Brooklyn Dodgers T-shirt." Bone looked up and the child was gone.

"I thought the building was sealed. We just searched it." He turned around to look at Loraine. "You see something, too?"

She nodded. "He was there for a second…then he was gone."

"Ho-ly crap," Bone muttered. "Brooklyn Dodgers."

"You mean the Los Angeles Dodgers, don't you?" Tiny was perplexed.

"Uh-uh. The Dodgers played in New York for years, until they moved to LA."

"When was that?"

"1958…the year the mill closed."

T-Bone stared at him for a moment and then began humming the theme song from *Twilight Zone.*

§§§

CHAPTER NINETEEN

GAINESVILLE

"All your cash, lady…I want it all." The robber pointed a Saturday night special .38 revolver at the cashier of Burk's Family Barbecue in the Northside strip mall on Highway 82.

"Please, don't shoot anybody…You can have all we got." The full-figured fifty year old woman at the register handed the twenty something man the cash from the register.

He waved his pistol at her and around the partially filled dining area. "No phone calls, hear?" The young man had a wicked grin on his face. "I know where you live."

She held up her hands in front of her. "No, please."

He backed toward the door. "Don't forget, no calls."

The robber opened the door just as a well-dressed older woman with a cane was about to come in. He snatched her purse from her hand and shoved her back where she screamed and fell heavily to the sidewalk.

A local cowboy had parked his pickup with his horse trailer hitched to the back in the large parking area in front of the shopping center. His horse was saddled for the day's work helping a friend gather cattle at a nearby ranch.

The thirty year old cowboy heard the woman scream, then saw her fall to the concrete as her assailant jumped on a motorbike parked in front of the barbecue restaurant.

He wheeled about, ran to the back of the trailer, unlatched the gate, swung it open and spoke to his horse, "Back up, son, back up."

The sorrel gelding backed out of the trailer and stood on the asphalt at the rear as the cowboy tightened up his cinch and swung deftly into the saddle.

He untied his lariat and built a loop as he saw the man on the motor bike tear out of the lot to the west and turn south.

The cowboy gigged his horse and squeezed him up into a gallop around the end of the strip of buildings and cut across toward the back street.

The well-trained cowhorse responded to the cowboy and headed the man on the bike just like a steer.

The gelding reached the edge of the street just as the robber on the motorbike sped past him right to left at thirty miles an hour.

The cowboy twirled the lariat over his head several times and expertly flipped a perfect houlihan loop that fell cleanly over the man's head and shoulders. The horse automatically rolled to his left as the cowboy jerked the slack and dallied his rope off on his saddlehorn.

The loop tightened around the robber's arms, pinning them to his sides and the young man was snatched from the seat of the bike when he reached the end of the rope.

Bone, Loraine, and Tiny Bone were driving past the strip mall headed to the trailer park on 82 and saw the cowboy on horseback take out after the man on the motorbike.

Bone turned the wheel to follow the biker down the side street. "Well, this looks like it's going to be interesting."

They witnessed the catch and watched as the biker flew from his bike backward and hit the pavement with a bone shattering thud.

"Oooh, that's gonna leave a mark," said Tiny as Bone pulled in behind the cowboy dragging the man back toward the barbecue restaurant.

The man snared in the loop, rolled first to his stomach, and then to his back as they crossed the parking lot and two curbs.

"Sure hope he did something bad," commented Loraine.

"Five'll get you ten, he did...That's a real cowboy that's got him...They live by a code. Long as there's one cowboy taking care of one cow…The cowboy ain't dead."

They pulled up behind the unfortunate man in the rope. He had large areas of exposed skin, strawberried, with holes torn in his clothes.

The woman whose purse he stole, shuffled forward and gave the man on the ground a couple of whacks with her cane. "Where's my purse, you…you, thievin' white trash?"

People were beginning to gather around the excitement as Bone turned the Thing around and drove back to the bike still lying in the street.

Tiny got out and picked up the woman's purse lying near the bike. "Guess we know what happened, now." He grinned.

They drove back to where the cowboy was stepping down from his saddle. His horse was keeping tension on the rope, not allowing the robber to get to his feet.

Bone showed his badge clipped to his belt as he walked up.

The cowboy pointed. "Feller there knocked this woman down an' took her purse…Hadn't oughta done that…ain't right…" He nodded his head once. "Don't tolerate it, don't tolerate it atall."

The cashier from the restaurant walked up. "He got all our cash, too."

Bone nodded to Loraine. She stepped over to the Thing, grabbed the mic from the radio. "Kilo 12-55 to dispatch. Come in Lauri."

"Dispatch, go ahead Loraine."

"Lauri, we have a 10-95, need a uniform unit at Northside strip mall."

"10-4, Laurie, this is Lima 24, I'm close, I'll take it."

"Roger that, 24."

"Garcia is on the way." Loraine hung up the mic.

Tiny patted the perp down and came up with the cheap .38. and the wad of cash from the restaurant in his pockets. "Armed robbery, too."

"It ain't loaded," said the man on the ground.

"Doesn't matter, Einstein, still a gun and the folks you robbed didn't know that...Oh, just for future reference...that can get you killed." Bone shook his head. "Time and effort will take care of ignorance...but stupid is forever."

"I need a doctor," the perp said.

"People in hell need a drink of water, too." Bone glanced down at the bleeding man.

Bone's cell rang. "Bone...Got something else, Doc?"

"Maybe, so, maybe not. Ascertained one thing."

"And that would be?"

"All the excision cuts on each vic were made by a left handed person...there is a difference in the angle of the cut between a lefty and a righty...Blew up some photos of the incision line on each vic...No question."

"Well, that's interesting, Doc. Much obliged." He punched his phone off.

GAINESVILLE PD

Stella ran through the list of phone calls made and received from Bernie's cell phone. She started two years back just like on his bank statements. "Well, well, that number's comin' up a lot...comin' an' goin'...Girl friend, maybe?"

Lacy, the receptionist, knocked on the door jam. "Stella, got a package for Bone."

"Just set it on his desk there, I imagine they'll be back soon as they check out the perp's residence."

"Can do." She set the shoe box size package on Bone's desk and turned around to go back to her desk up front.

GOLDEN YEARS MOBILE HOME PARK

Bone whipped into a driveway leading to a silver and blue single wide trailer with a navy blue awning over a small deck outside the front door.

"Kinda odd a guy as young as he was living in a retirement community." Loraine unbuckled her seat belt as Tiny stepped out and then held the passenger door open for her.

"Could be that he inherited the trailer from a parent or grandparent."

"Possibility. Hadn't thought of that." She stepped out onto the asphalt driveway. "Thank you, kind sir."

"My pleasure. Appreciate ya'll springin' for lunch. Those ribs were kinda good."

Bone scooted out of the driver's side. "That's why I always get a double-double. Brisket and ribs." He patted himself on the stomach.

"Eating with you two gorillas makes me feel like a fairy princess."

Bone laughed. "Uh-huh...Tinkerbell with D-cups...They say the way to a man's heart is through his stomach."

"If that's the case, you should marry your Big Green Egg."

T-Bone laughed. "Good one, Shortcakes." He held up his hand for a high five.

Loraine obliged and followed him and Bone up the steps to the wooden deck and front door.

"We gonna have to pick the lock?"

Bone shook his head. "Pay attention, little brother." He slipped his hand into his left front pocket and pulled out a key ring. "Behold...courtesy of Mister Bernie."

The detective looked around as if someone might be listening in. In a low voice, he said, "Snagged 'em before EMS tossed his carcass on the gurney."

"Slick one, bro. I'll remember that."

"Don't see any signs for alarm companies. Old Bern musta been a trusting soul. Know for sure he wasn't planning to have little Stella triple tap 'im…Therefore, I conclude the possibility of a booby trap is nil."

He went through the keys to find a probable one and slipped it in the door lock. It worked—he opened the door and counted to three before he stepped inside. Loraine and Tiny followed right behind him.

Bone flipped the light switch on, illuminated a well-appointed, but dated living room.

"Feel like I've been transported back to 1990. My Aunt Lucinda had the very same couch in Fort Worth." Loraine smiled.

Bone walked to the kitchen. "T-Bone, check it out. Lookin' for a long sharp knife. Use gloves if you find one. Also, and it's a long shot, but check the freezer for body parts."

Tiny nodded.

"What about me, Pard?"

"Find a desk or drawer or anyplace he might have kept notes."

"Okay, what's your job?"

"Me? Looking for a laptop or PC. Might have links to his personal contacts, et cetera. Shouldn't take long…Place ain't all that big."

Tiny went through the kitchen in three minutes. "Guys, the killer was no cook...Didn't own a chef knife or even a boning knife, and most of the cookware was old but barely used...Two frozen TV dinners in the fridge...ate out a lot."

Bone came out of the master bedroom with a laptop and a tower from a desktop. "Our guy must stream everything. There were no DVDs, no CDs...no computer discs whatsoever."

Loraine held a small fold-over checkbook. "Went through his little desk and could find no bills at all. Must pay on line."

"It's the new millennium. Let's haul butt back to the office and see what Stella's found."

As they stepped out on the porch, Bone spotted a Yamaha four wheeler on a small two-wheel trailer in the fenced-in backyard. He tilted his head that direction.

"Check out the wide tires on that bike. Ain't knobby and built for off road. That could be why we never found tracks leading to the body they found up near the Red."

Tiny agreed. "Could have driven off the trailer a quarter mile from where he entered the woods. No footprints at all."

"We can come back later and check it for DNA. I'm more interested in who he might have been associated with."

Bone set the computer down on a small table set beside a Weber charcoal grill. He locked the door and slipped the keys back into his pocket.

§§§

CHAPTER TWENTY

GAINESVILLE PD

Stella could hear Bone, Loraine, and Tiny in the hallway as they talked to Lacy.

"Package on your desk, Bone."

"Must be from a secret admirer."

"Or a Unibomber copy cat," said Loraine.

"Huh…If it's candy, don't ask for any."

They walked through the doorway as Loraine responded, "Might be poisoned anyway.

"How's it going, Little Bit, find anything?" Bone set the laptop and tower from Lipschitz's trailer on her desk.

She grinned and nodded. "I'd say…Got it all written up there on your desk next to your package."

"That's his stuff there, need to go through it." Bone picked up the box and shook it. "Nothing hard." He pulled out his knife again and carefully slit the paper and tape wrapping, set the box back on his desk and lifted the lid off.

There was a black lace bra inside lying on a bed of tissue paper. The bra was neatly cut between the cups.

"Son-of-a-bitch!"

Stella looked over from her seat at Loraine's computer the box. "What?"

Loraine and Tiny leaned over his desk to peer inside the box.

Bone took out a latex glove, put it on and lifted the two pieces of the bra out of the box.

Loraine brought her hand to her mouth. "Oh, my God!"

In the bottom of the box on top of the tissue paper was a cut and pasted note pieced together from magazines.

Bone read it aloud, *"Detective Bone, I thought you might want the matching bra one of my last subjects wore. I'm sorry that the cups no longer runneth over. I'm ready for some more white meat. Too bad I missed out on the little blonde. Maybe next time."*

Stella's chin hit her chest as all the color left her face.

Bone, Loraine, and Tiny exchanged looks...

GOVERNOR'S LOUNGE

Later that night, Bone, Loraine, Stella, Wanda, Tiny, Ginny Mac, Peach, Sheriff Brennan, and all the other officers who were not on duty were celebrating Stella's safe return.

It was *HAT NIGHT* at the Governor's Lounge. Everyone wore a mixture of 'unusual' hats.

The last to arrive was the captain. Vertis handed him a Napoleon style bicorne hat as he came in.

"Here David, this one suits your personality."

St. John grinned. "You really know how to hurt a guy, Vertis." He put the hat on, stuck his hand in his shirt, and strutted over to the table where Stella sat with a Sherlock Holmes hat on her head. He pulled out a chair next to her.

"Stella, just spoke to the D.A. and you've been no-billed by the Grand Jury...Justifiable Homicide. And I guarantee that the IAD will give you a 'Righteous Shooting' ruling...Congratulations. Actually I'm putting you in for a commendation."

Ginny stepped over and gave Stella a hug. "Way to go, girlfriend!"

"Wow, thanks Cap'n...Now when can I go back to work?"

"Dammit, Stella, would you chill? Look at your hands...they're still rope burned, an' you got scrapes an' bruises all over you...I can still see the knot on the back of your head. Stay on desk duty in the Investigative Unit...We still need the rest of that info...Give it a couple more days...please?"

She frowned. "All right...But it doesn't mean I have to like it."

Bone walked over from the bar with a galvanized funnel in his hand and he had a leather German WWI aviator's cap on his head.

"Hey, I bet anyone here ten dollars that they can't drop a quarter from their forehead into this funnel stuck into their belt...blindfolded."

Loraine looked up at the big man. "Dare's go first, Bone."

Bone stuck the funnel in his belt, tied a blue paisley bandanna around his eyes and leaned his head back.

He placed a quarter in the middle of his forehead, then slowly straightened his head up until the quarter fell off and dropped directly into the funnel with a cling.

Bone took the blindfold off. "Piece of cake...for the talented, that is. Who's gonna try next...Stella, Ginny?"

Tiny had an Abraham Lincoln stove pipe hat on. He got to his feet, stepped toward Bone, and his hat was knocked from his head by the ceiling fan. Tiny picked it up and grinned.

"No, let me do it. I'll take your money, Bone." He handed his hat to Loraine.

"Okey-dokey, brother."

Bone tied the bandanna around T-Bone's eyes and stuck the funnel down the front of his pants.

"Now tilt your head back." Bone placed the quarter on Tiny's forehead, reached over and grabbed a mug of beer from Stella's hand.

Bone allowed Tiny long enough to slowly bring his head forward before he emptied the full mug of beer into the funnel and quickly stepped back.

Tiny yelled, jerked the bandanna from his eyes, looked down at the large wet stain that covered the entire front of his pants and crotch and glared at Bone.

The entire bar roared in laughter.

"Damn you, Bone!"

Bone took off and ran around and through the tables...Tiny was right behind him.

Vertis charged out from the back of the bar with a broom. "Out, out, out! Get out of my bar, you knot heads!"

Bone headed toward the front door. He darted out as Vertis swatted Tiny across the back three times with the broom before he, too, could make it out.

A moment later, Bone barreled through the back door. He spun around and locked it behind him.

Vertis walked toward Bone, threatening him with the broom.

Bone held up his hands in surrender. "Kings X, Vertis."

A series of loud bangs reverberated through the building as Tiny hammered on the back door. "Damn you, Bone! This ain't fair!"

Outside, Tiny stepped around the corner where Bone's Thing was parked nose-in to the side of the building. He looked at it and grinned.

Inside, everyone stared at the front door as they watched for Tiny to come back in.

Bone's Thing had three flat tires. Air was still hissing from the valve stem of the fourth, Tiny looked at it with a satisfied grin, dusted his hands off, walked back around to the front door and entered.

Bone saw him come in and walked up good-naturedly. "Hey, T-Bone…no hard feelings?"

"Aw, you know me, brother, never hold a grudge any longer than it takes to get even…And you can quote me on that."

Bone turned his head and muttered sotto, but everyone could hear him, "Oh, crap."

The bar erupted in laughter again.

Captain St. John held up a bottle of Corona. "I want to make a toast…Here's to a job well done, by a helluva cop…Stella Johnson…Think Stella's now qualified to join *MOSS*."

Everyone in the club responded, "Here, here."

Stella had a confused look on her cute face. "What's *MOSS*?"

The captain looked down at her and winked. "Mystic Order of Secret…Uh…Stuff."

"How do I join?"

Wanda grinned. "You'll see during the initiation."

Stella rolled her amber gold eyes. "Oh, boy."

St. John held his bottle up again. "But, back to the matter at hand…We took one sick son-of-a-bitch off the streets and solved a string of murders at the same time."

Bone shook his head and frowned. "Don't think so Cap'n. Checked the delivery on that box and it was sent after Stella triple capped Lipschitz...No question in my mind he was hired help, muscle...His hands tell me no way in hell he could handle a scalpel with that kind of skill, and we found no trace of the excised breasts, or even blood, at his trailer house...Plus the doc says the cutter was left handed." He paused and looked around at the other cops. "The North Texas Butcher was right handed...Could tell that when we fought."

Loraine cocked her head and looked at him. "Think you're right, Pard...You said earlier that your gut was telling you something was wrong."

Bone nodded. "Always go with your gut."

They all looked at Bone quizzically, and then at each other...

§§§

CHAPTER TWENTY-ONE

BONE RANCH

"Mighty white of you to give me a ride home, brother…considering you let the air out of all my tires."

Tiny grinned and took a sip from his Shiner Bock. "Seemed like the thing to do at the time…no pun intended."

Bone nodded. "Gotta call Barthold in the morning to go over and air those puppies back up."

"How do ya'll keep from killin' each other?" asked Padrino from his rocking chair as he wiped the top of his bottle of Bud.

The three men sat on the wraparound porch of the one hundred and twenty year old house looking at the myriad stars twinkling like diamonds in the sky and having a beer out at the ranch after Bone and Tiny drove home from the Governor's Lounge.

"Getting even has nothing to do with love, Padrino," said T-Bone. "Say, you said you'd tell me about that person, Lucy, you mentioned at the mill…and about that empathy thing."

"All right, brother, but don't say I didn't warn you."

"Go for it."

Bone took a long draught of his beer. "It all started on April 17, 1897…"

Tiny frowned. "Say, what?"

"Just pay attention, grasshopper, and all will become clear."

He shook his head and took another drink of his Shiner. "Probably another one of your BS stories."

"All true, Tiny, I was there too."

The younger Bone brother arched his eyebrows and glanced over at Padrino.

"As I was sayin', on April 17, 1897, a spacecraft crashed at Aurora, Texas…Reported in the Dallas Morning News on April 19…look it up."

Tiny nodded. "I'll do just that."

"The locals gave the pilot a Christian burial in the town cemetery, and wrote on the headstone…*Not of this world*…Someone stole it in 1954."

"Uh-huh."

"Seems there was a survivor, a woman…Now, over five thousand years ago, the ancient Sumarians called her people the *Anunnaki*…meaning 'they who from the stars came'."

"You mean those people they made the carvings of were aliens?"

Bone nodded. "So it would seem. They've been visiting our planet for millennia…they're also called 'the Watchers'…more about that later…You getting all this?"

"So far."

"Well, seems they look just like us, or as Lucy said, we look just like them, only larger. They have been infusing their DNA into the most promising hominids on our planet starting over two million years ago...settling on the best, Homo Sapiens, which became us...Home Sapiens Sapiens."

Tiny's brow wrinkled. "Come back with that."

"You ought to be taking notes, T-Bone, there might be a quiz." Padrino smiled.

"Joy."

Padrino picked up the narrative. "Anyway, they travel here through an Einstein-Rosen bridge or wormhole, if you will, so they can get here in hours or even minutes...They have the technology to create one wherever it's needed.

"But not so with their radio. Their signals have to go through what Lucy termed, subspace, and are limited to the speed of light. Their planet, Tyrin..."

The big pit bull laying at Bone's feet, picked up his head at the mention of his name, then he laid it back down between his paws.

"...is thirty-two parsecs from here or about 117 light years. So it would take that long for her radio wave from her portable transmitter to get from

Earth to her planet to let them know she needed rescue."

Bone nodded at Padrino. "It's a good thing their life span is about 400 of our years, but they don't age when they travel through those wormholes, 'cause they're traveling faster than light. It took 117 of our years for them get the message and to come get her...She aged naturally while she was here."

Tiny shook his head. "I'm gettin' a headache. May need somethin' stronger than this beer."

Bone grinned. "You wanted to know...Well, long story short, Lucy was taken in by Cletus and Mary Lou Wilson as an abandoned mute child...Right here on this very ranch...They gave her an Earth name...*Lucy*, actually it was our great grandmother, US Deputy Marshal Fiona Miller, that named her...it was before she married great grandpa Sheriff Mason Flynn."

"You jest."

"Kid you not."

"So, how did you meet her?"

"Well, that's the thing. Captain St. John and I were out bird hunting and accidentally crossed on her property...She inherited the ranch from the

Wilsons when they both died in the great Spanish flu epidemic in 1918."

"But how did you get it?"

Bone nodded and took another sip of his Shiner. "Gettin' to that, don't get your panties in a wad...There were some bad guys with an energy company that wanted this place for that big gas play that's going on right now. They were harassing and threatening to burn her out...Had to deal with the situation so she would be here when her people came to get her."

"She said that our blood line..." He nodded at Padrino. "...was very strong as empaths, but didn't know how to use it yet...Lucy taught Padrino and me how to access the ability before she was rescued."

"And you can teach me?"

"Maybe...If I can ever get through that thick skull of yours."

"Bite me...So how did you wind up with this ranch?"

"In return for taking care of the bad guys and saving her life so she could get rescued, she signed this ranch, the title to that '29 Cord Cabriolet out in the barn, some gold and diamonds, and of course, we got her companion, Tyrin, here."

He raised his wide muscular head again and was rewarded by Bone ruffling his short ears.

"When can you teach me?"

"Well, we need to get this case wrapped up, so your mind can focus and is receptive to the ability…Like I said, it's in there." He pointed to Tiny's head. "Just have to figure out how to access it."

"You're not pullin' my leg, are you, brother?"

Padrino looked over at Bone. "Show him."

Bone took out his phone, swiped the screen and hit the tiny gray icon up in the right corner. In a brief moment, the air in front of the three men shimmered and the pixie-haired Lucy appeared—again, sans her helmet.

Tiny jumped up from his rocker and spilt some of his beer. "Holy cow!"

"Lucy, meet my…"

She smiled, crinkling her tiny nose. "I know…your baby brother, Eugene, better known as Tiny…How do you do, young man?"

"Ah…ah…ah…uh   fine…uh,   Ma'am…uh, Lucy."

"Just breathe, brother, just breathe."

"You're real, I mean, you're not, but…"

Padrino also grinned. "We know what you mean, T-Bone…Yes, she's a hologram and her image is being projected from her Watcher station in outer space."

"Oh, wow, I'm meeting an actual alien." He sat back down in his rocker.

Tyrin woofed and wagged his tail at her.

"Actually you could say we're your progenitors."

"Yeah, Padrino mentioned something about that."

"How did you know his name, Lucy?"

"My dear Bone, your mind is an open book to me…With more practice, you will be able to read others."

"Does that include me, too…uh, Lucy?"

She glanced at the younger Bone. "Of course."

"Well, thanks, Lucy. Just thought my baby brother should meet you…Not sure he was believing me."

"I know, Bone. I constantly read you…and you're right, you know."

"'Bout what?"

"There being someone behind the Butcher."

"Do you know who?"

"Bone, you know I don't do things that way…You'll figure it out."

Lucy waved good bye, the air shimmered again and her image disappeared.

Tyrin looked up at Bone and whined.

GAINESVILLE POLICE STATION

Tiny pulled into the parking lot a few seconds before Bone. He waited for him to unbuckle and get out. "Ride any better with new air in the tires?"

Bone grinned. "Of course…I like to change the air 'bout once a quarter, whether it needs it or not."

"Don't forget to check the blinker fluid, too. Those VWs are pretty high maintenance." Tiny winked.

"If you were wonderin'…it was worth it." The detective laughed. "You shoulda seen your face."

T-Bone started to answer, but his cell phone rang. He opened the app and saw it was his captain. He glanced at his brother as they walked toward the back door of the building. "It's my boss. Gotta take this."

He tapped the green phone icon and brought the phone to his ear. "Ranger Bone, how's it going Captain?"

Bone could pretty much figure out what was the gist of the conversation just from listening to Tiny's responses.

"We're almost wrapped up here...the murderer is dead. We performed a full CSI of the suspected murder scene and the perp's residence."

Tiny nodded as the captain explained his next assignment. "Uh huh...sixty-three cars? Yep, sounds like a large theft ring to me."

Bone looked on as Tiny covered the cell phone mic and mouthed, "Dallas."

"I understand, Captain. One thing we kept under wraps is the package sent to the man heading up the investigation."

Tiny rolled his eyes as the Captain droned on about the Dallas mayor and political pressure on the DPD. "I'm aware of that, sir, but the North Texas Butcher is still out there...at least the brains of it. They went so far as to taunt the lead investigator with a victim's bra and patchwork note."

Bone smiled to himself as his relationship to Ranger Tiny Bone was so neatly sidestepped.

"Yes, Captain. Noon tomorrow, come hell or high water...I'll be in touch." Tiny ended the call.

"So, I take it we've got a little over twenty-four hours to wrap this dog and pony show up before Cinderella has to hit the road."

"You could say that, but you should have used Prince Charming."

"Wouldn't want you to get a big head, little brother." Bone laughed. "Come on...Let's see what Little Bit came up with."

§§§

CHAPTER TWENTY-TWO

GAINESVILLE POLICE STATION

Tiny and Bone entered the break room and each grabbed a mug off the peg board. They filled them with Bone's special custom blend, grabbed two of Mom Tucker's donuts from the white cardboard box on the table, and headed down the hall to the Crime Investigator's Office.

Loraine and Stella were already seated at their desks. Bone and his brother took their seats.

"Aren't you two the eager beavers today." Bone took a sip of his coffee.

"Been here less than five minutes, you slackers."

Loraine took a sip from her mug. "Take it you got your tires aired up."

"Sure. Lucky T-Bone didn't knife 'em…this time."

"You mean he…" Loraine's mouth dropped.

"Hell, yes, back when he was in college." Tiny smiled broadly.

Bone chuckled. "Just a little Exlax in the brownies…some kiddos lack a sense of humor…Totally."

"Should have known he was up to no good, just before the homecoming game. The whole defensive line was embarrassed." Tiny's eyes narrowed.

"Remind me never to drop my guard around that brother of yours." Stella shook her head.

"Enough of old home week." Bone was still chuckling about his past deeds. "What's the skinny on ol' Bern?"

Stella opened the folder. "Well for starters, there was a pattern of cash distributions that were not from his employer beginning about the time the first vic disappeared. I gave the printouts to Loraine to confirm."

"Any ideas where the funds came from?" Bone took a bite of a chocolate glazed donut.

""Best I can tell, an account in the Cayman Islands...All handled by wire transfer."

Tiny frowned. "Dang it. Offshore banking...It's a bear to get those guys to cooperate and give up the account holder's info."

"Bummer, indeed." Bone took another bite of the pastry and washed it down with his stout java juice. "Just out of curiosity, how much was old Bernie boy taking in for each vic?"

Loraine crossed her arms. "Two grand."

"Can't friggin' believe it. Two grand?...That's it?" Bone shook his head. "What kind of monster kills a gorgeous young woman for pocket change?...Works out to one large per boob..."

Loraine shivered and Stella crossed her arms in front of her chest.

"Sorry ladies, My little big brother is short of sensitivity training for the year." Tiny gave Bone a hard look.

"For the year?" Loraine shook her head. "He's short for the decade. My partner is what the shrinks call...impulse control challenged."

Bone finished off the first donut and licked the icing from his index finger. "So, sue me."

He lifted the cover sheet to the paperwork on his desk. "Stella, my dear, you do good work...for a newbie." He noted a number highlighted in yellow.

"What's the deal with this one in magic marker?"

"He called it numerous times in the past three weeks as well as received calls from it."

"Did you find out whose name is it in?"

She nodded. "It's registered to Bernie Lipschitz." She smiled wanly. "A low end model from Radio Hut."

"So Bernie buys a burner phone and gives it to his handler."

"Guess so."

"You call it?" Bone raised one eyebrow.

Stella shook her head vigorously. "Didn't want to screw up the investigation." She shrugged her shoulders.

"You still got his phone?"

"Uh-huh." The blond bombshell slipped open her top desk drawer. She handed over an iPhone 8 that Peach had dropped off earlier.

Touching the killer's personal item sent a shiver down her spine.

Bone held it in his left hand and pushed the button to turn it on. As he waited for the phone to open up, he downed his first cup of coffee.

He put his mug on his desk and slid his right index finger over the screen. He tapped on the green icon and brought up the phone screen.

Tiny, Loraine, and Stella kept their eyes glued to the unit. Bone selected the keyboard and entered the number Bernie had called so frequently.

The letters *SAL* appeared as the number connected. Bone hit the speaker phone function. All four listened closely, scarcely daring to breathe.

"You have reached a number that has been disconnected or is no longer in service. Please check your directory and dial again."

"Crap...No cigar for you, sir." Tiny grinned. "Burner phone...odds are they ditched it when news broke of Bernie's recent departure."

"You saw something on the directory. What did it say?" Loraine was curious.

"Pard, did you read my mind?" Bone pointed a finger at her.

"No, dummy, I watched your face and saw a slight look of surprise."

He glanced at Stella. 'See that, kid? Good cop work...My poker face needs work." He turned back to Loraine. "The letters S-A-L. All caps. Nickname for Sally...Sal Mineo...Salmonella."

"You're no help."

"Sorry, Pard. I wanted it to be the brains behind the operation."

"And what exactly would you have said to them? 'We know you did it. We have you surrounded? Give up!'"

"We'll never know, will we?" Bone crossed his arms and frowned. "I'm fresh out of coffee."

Tiny looked somewhat disappointed. "Plenty of coffee in the break room...Is that all ya'll have on Lipschitz?"

Bone nodded. "So far...Tell you what. Have some other ideas..." He pointed at his brother. "T-bone, do a full-on legal history of our man, even so far back as juvenile...Traffic tickets, vagrancy, minor in possession...you name it. Want it all."

He turned to Loraine. "Double D, get me any contract he ever signed, liens, tax records, real estate...the works. There is something out there tying him to his handler. Don't know what it will be until I see it."

"I'll get hoppin' on it."

"How about me, Bone?" Stella looked sad at being left out.

"Ain't forgot you, blondie. Social media autopsy. Every tweet, Instagram, Facebook, Pinterest, You Tube...whatever you younger folks do. Find it. Categorize it...Put links in a secure email for my work account."

"It'll take a while." She frowned.

"Rome was not built in a day." Bone made a face. "Jeez. I'm starting to sound like my mother."

"Kinda look like her, too." Tiny chuckled.

"Watch it, buster." Bone grabbed his coffee mug and got to his feet.

Tiny already had his laptop opened up and in the FBI's NICS database. "What are you gonna do while we are nose to the grindstone?"

"The Duke of Detectives will be cogitating while he gets a refill of Black Rifle…On a whim, gonna do some preliminary work on that new doctor, Stanley Albert Landrum…SAL? Don't believe in coincidences." He ambled to the door.

Loraine rolled her eyes. "Go get 'em, Duck."

Bone strolled back in a few minutes later. "Hey guys, just for the record, saw Chief Anderson walking down the hall. Guess you didn't make him a eunuch after all, Stella."

"Don't remind me. Still feel terrible about that." Her forehead wrinkled.

"Not as bad as he did…guarantee it." Tiny grinned.

"True, that."

Bone had an idea as he sat down and took a second sip of his brew. *Never did find out what year Pat graduated from Denton High.*

He sat his mug down and opened his laptop. He

Googled the TV station in Ardmore and checked out the links to the members of the news team.

Bone mumbled to himself as he continued, "Pat Jenkins graduated UNT in 2007 with a degree in photo journalism. That would likely make her a 2003 high school senior."

He clicked on a link to Lisanne Miller. Some were pics, obviously glamour shots, others of her on the scene of dramatic news coverage and one caught his eye.

Lisanne stood next to a tall shapely blond with a killer figure. "Get out of town...My little news hound knows Chrystal Towers."

He read the blurb beneath the publicity still. "Huh? They film the cooking show webcast in the Ardmore Studios of KTXP...Whooda thunk it?"

Armed with that information, Bone pulled up an on-line version of the Denton High School annual for 2003. He went straight to the index at the back.

"Here we go. Patricia Jane Jenkins...Pages 44, 128, 184, 205."

Bone scrolled back to the senior pic. "That's her all right...with long straight hair. All the chicks wore it that way, I see."

He went back to the index. "Let's see what old Bernie looked like. Huh...Only on pages 47 and 219."

Quickly, he scrolled back his senior picture. Bernie wore his hair in a flat top and was in a white button down shirt with a black tie. "Yep. Nothin' unusual. Just a big hunk of junior sociopath."

Bone's cell rang with the familiar strains of the *William Tell Overture*. He answered, "Bone, what's up Peach?...You don't say?...My...My...Thanks, babe, owe you one...Laterbye." He punched his phone off.

"Just for the hell of it, what's on page 219?" The cursor brought up the computer science club. "Geek city. Pocket protectors. Glasses. There's old Bern standing next to a tall, skinny chick. Well, he weighs about 250 in high school...Hard to say if she's really skinny."

Bone scanned the list of the twenty members. There was Bernard Lipshitz. The name of the girl beside him caught his eye. *Sarah Lipshitz.*

"What the hell?"

Bone raced through the pages back to the index. *Sarah Anne Lipschitz, freshman, pages 174 and 219.*

He slammed the cursor to the left arrow and whipped back to the ninth grade freshman class. His eyes locked on the fifteen year old girl. "Couldn't be."

Bone pulled out his cell phone. Using the camera function, he zoomed into the young brunette's picture and made it five times as large.

He sat there for a moment, shaking his head. "I'll be a suck egg mule…"

He looked up and said to the others, "Back in a few, ya'll, gotta make a head call."

The big man got to his feet and took his cell with him as he headed out the door.

Ten minutes later, Bone strode back in.

Tiny looked up. "Took you long enough…Shake it more'n three times, you're playin' with it."

Bone grinned. "Speaking from experience, little brother?" He grabbed his hat from the hook on the wall. "Saddle up, *muchachos*. Think we found our mastermind."

§§§

CHAPTER TWENTY-THREE

GAINESVILLE PD PARKING LOT

"What say we all go in my Thing?"

Tiny glanced over at his brother. "Where're we goin?"

Bone grinned. "You'll see…Get in."

T-Bone got in the front as before, with Loraine in the back. Bone cranked up, drove out of the lot and to the Interstate, three blocks from the station. He headed north.

Tiny turned his head around to his right and mouthed to Loraine, "Any idea what he's doin'?"

She shook her head and shrugged.

TELEVISION STATION KTXP

Forty minutes later, they pulled into the parking lot of KTXP.

There was also a plain detective's unit from the Ardmore PD parked there. A plainclothes cop got out as Bone parked next to him.

"Good timin', Bone,"

"Not much traffic this time of day...Dan, this is my partner, Inspector Loraine Rodriguez and my baby brother, Texas Ranger Tiny Bone...Guys, meet one of Ardmore's finest, Detective Dan Martelle."

He nodded. "Loraine..." Dan looked back at Bone. "Baby brother?"

"Two peas in a pod," commented Loraine.

Martelle shook his head. "God help us."

"See you've worked with Bone before." Loraine grinned.

The detective nodded. "Several times."

Bone looked back at Dan. "Get it done?"

"Right here." He patted the front of his sport coat over the inside pocket.

"What are we doin' here." Tiny looked puzzled.

"You didn't tell 'em?"

Bone grinned at Dan and shook his head. "Wanted it to be a surprise."

"Damn you, Bone." Loraine backhanded him across the chest. She looked at the Ardmore detective. "He does this all the time."

"Keeps you on your toes, Pard…and your mind open and working." He pointed to the door of the station. "Shall we?"

"Might as well, we're here," replied Dan.

"I will tell you this…" Bone looked at Loraine and Tiny. "…since we don't have any jurisdiction in Oklahoma, called my old pal Dan here to get a local warrant so we can make our arrest when I went to make a head call…Be easy enough to do an extradition later."

Dan opened the front door, and the men moved aside to let Loraine enter first.

"Goodness, thank you, gentlemen...You too, Bone."

He gave her a fake smile, and then approached the front desk and the slightly overweight receptionist with light brown hair. "Detective Bone to see Lisanne Miller..." He glanced down at her name plate on the desk. "...Barbara."

A look of temporary fear flashed across the girl's face. "Uh, may I tell her what this is regardin'?"

"No...Just tell her I'm here."

"Uh, yes, sir...Just a moment." She punched a button on her intercom. "Miss Miller, there's a..." She glanced up at the man towering over her. "...a Detective Bone here to see you."

A pleasant and familiar on-camera voice came back over the speaker. "You don't say? Interesting...I'll be right out, Barbara."

She looked back up and started to speak.

"We heard."

The three glanced down the hallway to see the very attractive Lisanne striding their way.

She held out her hand. "Detective Bone, what do I owe the pleasure." Lisanne looked over at

Detective Martelle. "Am I under arrest or something?"

Bone's grin spread across his face. "Did you do something that you should be arrested for?"

Her dazzling, perfect smile flashed back. "I'll never tell...So, how can I help you?"

"Why don't we go down to your offices...I assume your camera girl, Pat, is here?"

"She is...why?"

"Let's just go see her...shall we?"

Lisanne had a puzzled look on her face as she turned and led the way back down the hall to the on-camera talent offices next to the soundstage.

Bone looked at Lisanne before they entered. "By the way, you're not left handed are you?"

She returned the look. "No."

There were several monitors around on the walls where the network feeds were currently being aired. The Ardmore station was live only for the local news, weather, and sports—plus the occasional programs of local interest.

They entered and walked over to Pat's desk.

"Pat, why don't you get your camera and Lisanne you grab a mic."

"What's this all about, Detective?" asked Lisanne.

Bone looked down at her with a wry grin. "How would you like the biggest, totally exclusive, scoop of your life?"

"Do I get to know what it concerns first?"

Bone shook his head. "Uh-uh."

Lisanne glanced at Loraine and Tiny.

Loraine shrugged her shoulders. "Don't look at us...we don't know either." She glanced askance at Bone, and then at Detective Martelle.

"I sorta do, but only a piece of it," commented Dan.

The big man just smiled like a cat that ate the canary. "All things come to he who waits...Long as he works like hell while he waits."

Loraine snapped a glance at him. "Do what?"

Bone turned back to Lisanne. "Where are your webcast studios?"

"We only have one."

He nodded. "Ya'll grab your gear...and lead on."

Pat got up from her desk, walked over to some large metal shelves against a wall and picked up her steadycam, and then handed Lisanne her wireless mic after checking the batteries.

"I suggest you be rolling when we walk in the room."

"Bone, if this is some sort of a gag, I swear, I'll…"

"No gag, Pretty…You're gonna want to hug my neck when this is all through."

"Doubt that, but I'll go along…for now. This way."

She led the way again back down the hallway to a set of double doors, paused outside and looked at Pat and blew across her mic.

"Rolling…We have sound," Pat said softly.

Bone opened the right side of the doors and they all entered…

GAINESVILLE PD

Captain St. John walked into the Crime Investigator's Unit office. "Where the hell is Bone an' them?"

Stella looked up from her desk and shrugged her shoulders. "No clue. They left about forty-five minutes ago…He just said 'saddle up, *muchachos*, think we've found our mastermind', an' they boogied…He's got me checking all the social info on the perp."

"That's it?"

"He was doin' some stuff on his computer, got a call from Peach, then he said, 'Couldn't be', an' then, 'I'll be a suck-egged mule'. He made a head call, came back an' they left."

St. John walked over to Bone's computer, woke it up and looked at the last few screens he had gone to. He shook his head and grinned. "Only Bone."

KTXP

They stopped just inside the door. Chrystal Towers was creating one of her dishes on the set in front of two cameras, one for a master or wide shots, and the other for close-ups.

"Our dish for today is Meat Lover's Pot Pie." She scooped some diced meat from her cutting board into a stainless steel pot.

Bone elbowed Dan. The Ardmore detective handed him a folded document from his inside coat pocket.

The tall strikingly attractive blonde looked up as the group entered, "What is this? I'm in the middle of live show."

Bone stepped forward grinning. "Well, your audience should get a real kick out of this...Chrystal Towers, aka, Sarah Ann Lipschitz." He held up the document. "We have a warrant for your arrest for conspiracy to commit murder and desecration of a corpse after the fact." He nodded to Martelle.

The detective stepped up to Chrystal, turned her around and snapped his cuffs on her wrists behind her back. "You have the right to remain silent. Anything you say can and will be used against you in a court of law. You have the right to an attorney. If you cannot afford an attorney, one will be provided for you. Do you understand these rights I have stated?"

"What's going on?" She glared at Bone, and then at Martelle. "Are you crazy? I'll have your badge for this."

"Nice try Sarah, but you made a little mistake," said Bone.

"What are you talking about?"

He had his enigmatic grin on his face. "You inadvertently left a hair at the crime scene where you so deftly excised the breasts from your victims in the cafeteria at the old Johnson mill. Seems it was an exact mitochondria DNA match to the North Texas Butcher's hair...your brother, Bernie Lipschitz...except that it was bleached."

"No! No! You're lying!" She tried to twist away from Martelle, but to no avail.

"Plus I feel confident we'll find other incriminating evidence..."

Bone walked over to the Yeti cooler on the floor next to her prep table, pulled on a set of his latex gloves, and opened it. He took several Ziplock bags of diced meat out of the cooler and laid them on the table.

"Pard, you want to get pics of these?"

"My pleasure." Loraine took a number of pictures with her cell phone of the baggies.

Bone looked back at Sarah. "...What do you bet some of..." He looked at the bags. "...if not all, turn out to be mostly human breast tissue?"

Both Pat and Lisanne's eyes were big as saucers—their chins on their chests. The professional newscaster quickly overcame her shock and turned to the camera.

"This is Lisanne Miller reporting live from our studios in Ardmore, Oklahoma. You have just witnessed what has to be a first…A live on-camera arrest of a suspected serial murderer or in this case, murderess…"

A scream of pure anguish escaped from Sarah as she sank to her knees on the floor.

§§§

EPILOGUE

GAINESVILLE PD
CRIME INVESTIGATION UNIT

Bone finished the last line of his crime report, and then hit, PRINT. "That ought to do it."

He turned his head and watched as the pages dropped into the tray from the humming laser-jet printer.

When the last of the two copies of the fourteen page report was completed and collated, Bone removed them, stapled each together and stacked them on his desk.

He picked up his commemorative ceramic USMC cup, took a sip of the coffee and made a face. "Ugg, cold."

Bone got to his feet, strode to the break room. Lacy, the twenty-four year old receptionist was setting a box of still warm donuts from Mom Tucker's on the counter. The enticing aroma of fresh donuts rapidly filled the area when she opened the lid.

"Ah, an angel of mercy."

Lacy turned and looked at Bone as he came in the room. "Try to save some for everybody else, Bone."

He feigned a hurt look while he filled his cup. "Me? Would I eat them all?"

"Yes," was all she said as she left to go back to her desk at the front.

Bone watched her leave. "I resemble that remark."

"I know," she replied over her shoulder.

"Don't touch those, Bone."

His hand froze in midair over the donuts as he turned his head to look at St. John striding in from the hallway.

"At least not until I have mine."

"Why is everybody picking on me?"

"Because you deserve it," said Loraine as she followed the captain through the door.

Bone refilled his cup while St. John took two donuts and placed them on a napkin.

The captain took a bite of one of the glazed donuts and looked at Bone again. "You want to tell me how the hell you figured out that woman on the webcast show was the brains behind the butcher?"

Bone grabbed one of the chocolate covered donuts and took a large bite. "All in the report, Cap'n." He blew across the steaming coffee, licked the rim of his cup and took a sip.

"But, what led you to make the connection between the butcher and a TV personality?"

Bone shrugged. "In the report…Everything is in the report…Spent two hours huntin' and peckin' this morning…before anyone else was in, to write it."

"So, where is this phantom report?"

"On my desk."

"Damn you, Bone, I..."

"Got one for me, too?" Tiny walked in and went straight to the donut box.

"Of course, brother. Just waitin' on you to get here...You were still snoozing when I left the ranch this morning."

"Need my beauty sleep."

"Got that right...come on, T, get thee behind me." Bone picked two more donuts out of the box and headed back to his office.

Tiny, followed by Loraine, and then the captain, trailed Bone into the investigator's room.

Bone set his cup and donuts on his desk, picked up the reports, handed one to St. John, and the other to Tiny. "Here you are, gentlemen...Enjoy."

"We gotta get together more often, brother."

Tiny and Bone gave each other back slapping bear hugs.

"Think Cooke County can stand it?"

"Probably not," muttered Loraine.

"Now, I got errands to run...Gotta pick up some fixings for tonight."

"What's tonight?" asked Loraine.

"Making dinner for Lisanne out at the ranch." He lifted his eyebrows twice, ala *Magnum P.I.*

Loraine's dark eyes flashed momentary fire at the big man as he turned and headed out the door.

Tiny had a wry grin on his face as he wagged his finger at her. "Don't forget, I get to be best man."

"Out! Out! You big lug...Just get out!" Loraine threw a plastic cup of pencils at T-Bone's back as he scooted out the door, giggling.

St. John looked at her with a puzzled expression. "What was he talking about?"

Loraine spun around, jerked out the chair at her desk and sat down heavily. "Nothing."

BONE'S RANCH

A burgundy Lexus sport coupe pulled up outside the white picket fence as the big golden orb settled just below the western horizon. Tyrin barked and charged to the front gate. The stocky, muscular dog took up an aggressive stance, his teeth bared.

"Down, boy," Bone called out as he stepped out of the front door. "It's okay...She's our guest."

The pit bull immediately changed his attitude and began to wag his tail.

Lisanne stepped out of the driver's side carrying a metallic silver-colored sack in her left hand. She wore a pair of formfitting black leggings and a royal blue long-sleeved cashmere sweater with a modest V neck. A tiny gold chain hung around her slender neck, with a single white pearl on an elegant gold drop. It matched the two custom-made earrings that dangled an inch below her earlobes.

Her hair was freshly coifed, her makeup camera ready—Lisanne looked like a million bucks.

"Welcome to my humble abode, pretty lady. Don't you look spectacular tonight." Bone opened the gate to the picket fence as Tyrin danced eagerly at his feet. "Don't worry 'bout him. He's okay once he finds out that you are no danger to us."

"Thank you, sir. You clean up quite well yourself."

Bone had put on a pair of black wool slacks, a silk turtleneck in a deep wine color and a silver sports coat with a burgundy scarf folded neatly in the left pocket. A pair of black Luchese caiman skin boots finished off his outfit.

Lisanne smiled broadly as she stepped through the gate and glanced down at the pit bull. "Hi, there, big boy. What's your name?...Okay if I pet him?"

"Sure...Tyrin likes women more than men."

She rubbed behind his ears. "Interesting name. How did you come up with that?"

Bone shook his head. "His previous owner, Lucy, gave him that...She moved away and left him with me. Couldn't have pets in, her, uh...new place."

Bone's explanation was mostly true—leaving out a tiny few details like Lucy was an extraterrestrial fighter pilot and was standing guard as a Watcher between Earth and the star we happen to call the sun.

They walked to the house, and Bone held the door open for her.

"Smells great. Is that marinara sauce home made?"

"Yes, Ma'am. Been simmering for a couple hours. Would you like a drink before dinner?"

"Please call me Lisanne. Ma'am reminds me of my mother...Almost forgot...brought you a little present...Hear you like tequila."

"Bingo. The investigative reporter did her homework."

"It's just a little token of appreciation. Can't tell you how much it means to me that you gave me that scoop on Chrystal...It's still one of the top stories being played on all the major news networks. On-line hits have exceeded twenty million."

She handed him the sack.

Bone pulled out a box containing a hand-blown bottle of Gran Patron Burdeos. His eyes widened and sparkled as he gave her a look of surprise. "Wow, girl. You really know how to show appreciation."

"You ain't seen nothin' yet, cowboy." She winked, smiled and ran the tip of her tongue over her perfectly white upper teeth.

"By the way, you have to tell me how you knew Chrystal was behind the north Texas killings."

Bone grinned. "Well, I could bore you with a lot of detective, legalese jargon and superior investigative skills, but let's say that it was mostly SWAG."

"SWAG? Am I supposed to guess what that means?"

"Scientific Wild-Assed Guess."

RECIPE FOR MURDER

NORTH TEXAS MEDICAL CENTER

A pair of hands in light blue surgical gloves removed an opaque plastic bag from the freezer in the hospital lab.

The person opened the bag, removed a complete, intact female breast from a mulatto woman and laid it inverted on the prep table.

There were already a series of slides placed side-by-side next to the feeder tray of the hospital's electron microscope.

The skilled, expert technician held a scalpel in the left hand and deftly sliced paper-thin samples from the mammary tissue, and from the surrounding fat tissue—mounted them on the slides with Safranin O stain for one and Janus Green B for the other and covered them with glass slips.

A latex gloved right hand pressed the start button and the machine loaded the prepared slides. Immediately the highly detailed, respective images appeared on the large monitor.

"Ah…That's what I was looking for," commented the doctor.

§§§§§

PREVIEW
OF THE NEXT EXCITING

BONE & LORAINE ADVENTURE

SIN NO MORE

BY

Ken Farmer & Buck Stienke

CHAPTER ONE

COOKE COUNTY
CR 1201

"I'm so ready to get home...Thought Stella was goin' to wear us to a nub working on that new routine," said Maria Sanchez from the back seat.

"Yeah, she is so like obsessed," Lashandra Brewer commented from the front passenger seat of Patty Hellenger's 2014 Camero.

Patty drove, Cassie Lightman sat next to Maria in the back. All the high school girls were drinking beer.

"Totally. I think she just needs a good lay," added Cassie.

They all laughed as a car passed going in the opposite direction.

Patty glanced to her left. "That's Reverend Carmichael's car."

Lashandra giggled. "Wonder where he's goin' this time of night?"

"Probably to Oak Ridge for booze before they close at ten," replied Maria.

They laughed again.

Patty put her beer between her knees started texting on her cell phone with her thumb while she drove. She glanced down at her screen for a moment.

"Patty! Watch out!" screamed Cassie.

Patty looked up just in time to see a man and a bicycle lying in the road directly in front of the car. She slammed on the brakes.

They all screamed, but it was too late. She ran over the cyclist and the bike. There were two distinct thumps as first the front wheels hit the man and bike, and then the rear ones did the same.

Oh, God! You hit him! Stop! Stop!" screamed Maria.

Laxhandra panicked. "No! No!...We've been drinkin'!...Go, Go!"

Patty yelled, "I've got to stop!"

"You can't, you can't...we'll all go to jail and get kicked off the team! It's too late to help him...Get out of here!" countered Lisandra.

Patty stepped on the gas as she looked in her rearview mirror at the man in the road—tears rolled down her cheeks.

MOSS LAKE MARINA

Reverend Carmichael's car pulled to a stop in the dark parking lot at the marina and the driver got out. The car was parked facing another vehicle.

A shadowy individual stood in front of the other vehicle. One person knelt down. The other shot him in the forehead—the body fell forward.

The shooter stepped around to the back door of his car, opened it, took out a blanket, and walked forward to the driver's door of Carmichael's car. The person opened it, reached in and popped the trunk lever under the dash.

The shadowy individual walked back to the body, bent down, rolled the body over and took out a large knife…

CR 1201

A few miles down the road, Patty pulled to the side of the road. She rested her forehead on the top of the steering wheel for a moment. Then Patty grabbed her flashlight from the side door pocket and got out.

"Got to check for any damage…My dad'll kill me if anything's wrong."

The rest of the girls also got out, walked to the front of the car with Patty and looked for damage.

She shined the light around. "Don't see anything…Ya'll?"

Maria knelt down. "Oh, God, what are we going to do?"

Cassie glanced over at her. "Will you quit whinin'."

SIN NO MORE

MOSS LAKE

A bass boat skimmed across the glassy smooth lake under the pale light of a half moon until it was out of sight of the marina—it slowed to a stop, the wake pushed it forward another ten feet.

The shadowy person pulled a body over to the gunwale, held on to the blanket and rolled it into the water. Then they put the blanket down, picked up two cinder blocks that were tied to the body's feet and threw them overboard.

The body rapidly disappeared beneath the black surface.

A cell phone fell from the dead man's belt holster and fluttered to the bottom.

MOSS LAKE

Nestled in the rolling Texas hills, a short fifteen minute drive from Gainesville, lay a spring fed picturesque lake that covered some 380 acres of the bucolic countryside.

Summertime would find the lake busy with fishermen, skiers and jet skis enjoying the recreational aspects of the cool waters.

But once the night became longer and the temperature dropped, the lakeside vacation homes were empty and the lake became significantly quieter.

Three days later, Captain David St. John of the Gainesville PD and Doctor Burton Fisk, County Medical Examiner, were jigging for striper bass from St. John's boat.

Fisk flipped his Advantage Jawbreaker Bladed jig out to the side of the boat. "Got any leads on that hit and run I processed the other day?"

"I wish. What was the deal with the missing finger?"

"Looked like his left pinky was torn off when he was hit."

"Well, it wasn't found at the scene...Maybe an animal got it.

Fisk reeled his jig in and flipped it back out. "Make a quick snack...Any news on that missin' preacher?"

St. John tied a Booyah Melee Viberating jig on his line. "Nothin' yet. We've got out a

BOLO…Looks like he dropped off the face of the earth…When it rains, it pours."

He cast his new jig out about forty feet, let it sink to the bottom, then started popping it back toward the boat. After a couple of 'jigs', the tip of the rod bent.

"Whoa! Got somethin'." St. John set the hook.

He lifted the tip of his rod high and then down to take up the slack, reeling as he did so.

The doc looked at the rod. "Nah. Looks like you got a log or old tire."

"Think you're right. Definitely not a fish…But, I'm damn sure hung on somethin'."

He continued to lift and reel, lift and reel, until the line slowly came in. After a moment, a dark shape appeared just under the murky water. It slowly came to the surface and rolled over.

A pasty white face broke the surface of the water—the eyes were open and glazed over. A bullet was in the middle of the forehead.

Fisk leaned forward. "My God!"

The captain pursed his lips. "Looks like we found the missing preacher…Better mark this spot on the GPS so Stella and Moomer's dive team can find it…See if anything else is down there."

GAINESVILLE PD
EVIDENCE EXAMINING ROOM

Bone and Loraine were carefully going over a mangled bicycle lying on a table.

Loraine held a magnifying glass. "Look at this black material here on the frame.

Bone looked at the black mark then at the right pedal. "Uh-huh…There's a trace of white paint on this pedal…betcha it's from the oil filter. This bike wasn't struck by a vehicle." He glanced over at Loraine. "It was already prone when it was run over. Which means that the rider was probably also prone since there were no broken bones in the legs…Fisk said COD was punctured lungs…"

Bone looked up as the department forensics technician, Peach Presley, a 5'10" beauty from Georgia, passed by the door on the way to the restroom.

Bone quickly opened a drawer in a desk, took out a tin of black shoe polish and headed to the door.

"Where are you going?"

He grinned as he walked out into the hallway. "Gotta run an errand...meet you back in our office."

Bone walked rapidly down the hall, looked back in the direction of the restrooms, and turned into Peach's forensics lab.

He quickly crossed to Peach's binocular counter microscope, opened the tin of shoe polish, ran the tip of his finger across the black wax, and then rubbed the wax around the rim of one of the eyepieces. He repeated the process on the other one, sealed the tin and quickly exited the door.

Bone passed Peach just as she was coming out of the restroom.

"Morning, Peach. Everything come out all right?"

"Bless your tiny little heart, Bone. You really know how to talk to a lady."

He gasped. "We got ladies in this building?...Dang, nobody tells me nothing."

Peach looked over her shoulder. "That's two, Bone."

He giggled as he turned into the Crime Investigator Unit office.

The lead detective walked over to Loraine's desk.

"Say, have you gotten the tox screen on that hit and run from Peach yet?"

Loraine looked up from her laptop. "No, she said she'd have it this morning…" She got to her feet. "Let's go down to her lab and check."

"Lead on, McGruff."

They exited the door into the hallway and walked down to the lab where Peach was bent over the microscope fiddling with the focus knob.

"Peach, do we have the tox screen on that 03 yet?" asked Loraine.

She didn't look up from the microscope. "On my desk…He was definitely intoxicated. Point two nine…Well over twice the legal limit. No other drugs." She looked up. "I'm flabbergasted he could even keep that bicycle upright.

"He didn't, we believe he was passed out, lying in the road when he was run over," said Bone.

Loraine leaned forward. "What's wrong with your eyes?"

"Excuse me?"

"Got a mirror?"

SIN NO MORE

Peach took out her compact from her purse laying on the counter. She opened it and looked at her face.

"Damn you, Bone!"

"Durn girl, guess we'll have to call you Rocky Raccoon from now on."

"Swear to God, Bone, speakin' of coons..."

"I know, what I can't screw up, I crap on."

Bless your pea brain, Bone, somebody told you...You realize you're three gallons of crazy in a two gallon bucket...don't you?"

§§§

BLACKSTAR ENIGMA by T.C. Miller

HISTORICAL FICTION WESTERN
THE NATIONS by Ken Farmer and Buck Stienke
HAUNTED FALLS by Ken Farmer and Buck Stienke
HELL HOLE by Ken Farmer
ACROSS the RED by Ken Farmer and Buck Stienke
BASS and the LADY by Ken Farmer and Buck Stienke
DEVIL'S CANYON by Buck Stienke
LADY LAW by Ken Farmer
BLUE WATER WOMAN by Ken Farmer
FLYNN by Ken Farmer
AURALI RED by Ken Farmer
COLDIRON by Ken Farmer
STEELDUST by Ken Farmer
BONE by Ken Farmer
BONE'S LAW by Ken Farmer
BONE & LORAINE by Ken Farmer
BONE'S GOLD by Ken Farmer
BONE'S PARADOX by Buck Stienke
BONE'S ENIGMA by Ken Farmer
SILKE JUSTICE by Ken Farmer
SILKE'S QUEST by Ken Farmer

SY/FY
LEGEND of AURORA by Ken Farmer & Buck Stienke
AURORA: INVASION (Book #6 in the BEF) by Ken Farmer & Buck Stienke

HISTORICAL FICTION ROMANCE
THE TEMPLAR TRILOGY
MYSTERIOUS TEMPLAR by Adriana Girolami
THE CRIMSON AMULET by Adriana Girolami
TEMPLAR'S REDEMPTION by Adriana Girolami

MYSTERY/SUSPENSE
RECIPE for MURDER by Ken Farmer & Buck Stienke

Coming Soon

HISTORICAL FICTION WESTERN
McGRATH by T.C. Miller
SILKE'S RIDE by Ken Farmer

HISTORICAL FICTION ROMANCE
DAUGHTER of HADES by Adriana Girolami
ZAMINDAR and the LADY by Adriana Girolami

SY/FY
ANTAREAN DILEMMA by T.C. Miller

MYSTERY/SUSPENSE
SIN NO MORE by Ken Farmer & Buck Stienke

Thanks for reading *RECIPE for MURDER.* If you enjoyed it, I would really appreciate a review on Amazon. Our Author Pages are:
www.amazon.com/Ken-Farmer/e/B0057OT3YI
www.amazon.com/Buck-Stienke/e/B0057XZNKW

Personally autographed books available at our web site:
Web page: www.timbercreekpress.net

TIMBER CREEK PRESS